# A Desert Romance

A Hearts of Woolsey Novel – Book 2

## Savannah Hendricks

Grand Bayou Press

Library of Congress Control Number: 2022912244

ISBN Paperback 978-1-7344553-5-9

EBOOK B09P6P2LDH

For Film and TV Rights – GrandBayouPress@protonmail.com

Editor: Krista Dapkey - www.kdproofreading.com

Cover ST Adobe Stock with design by Savannah Hendricks

# A DESERT ROMANCE

Annually, 10% of the proceeds from the sale of this book, and all Savannah's books are donated to dog rescue organizations.

**READING IS BETTER WITH A DOG ~ Savannah**

# Contents

# Welcome to Woolsey

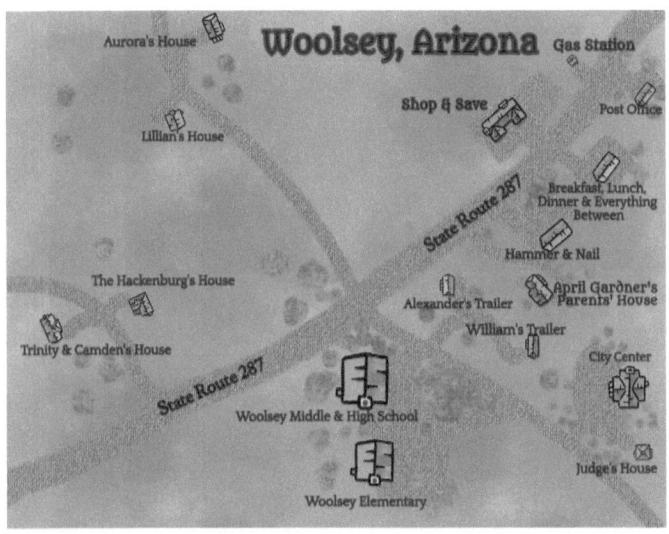

## Cast of Characters

*Gavin Hart* - long time neighbor of Mama & Elizabeth
*Aurora Easton* - Trinity's best friend
*Mike Easton* - Aurora's husband
*Willa Easton* - daughter to Aurora & Mike
*Ava Easton* - daughter to Aurora & Mike
*Trinity Moore* - teacher

# SAVANNAH HENDRICKS

*Camden Moore* - teacher
*Jolie Moore* – Trinity & Camden's daughter
*Elizabeth Dunn* - Judge
*Alexander Adams* - librarian
*William Adams* - guard at the city center/Alexander's dad
*Sydney Hernandez* - post office employee
*Lillian Taylor* - Trinity's Mom
*R. J. Smith* - owns Hammer & Nail
*Charlie Tow* - owns Shop & Save
*Ezra Hackenberg* - firefighter
*Wyatt Hackenberg* - firefighter
*Jasmine & Jeter Hackenberg* - Ezra & Wyatt's children

This book is dedicated to MacGyver, who passed during the final rewrites and edits of this story. I was not sure I could finish and push forth to keep writing—this or any other story—but not doing so would've meant that every second, minute, and hour of not being with you to write would've been for nothing. I would've lost both you and the story, and that would've been a disservice. For my little Mac-a-Boo, you loved me like nothing I've ever known, and I promise to honor you properly and bring attention to canine epilepsy.

# Chapter 1

## Aurora

The aroma and steam rose from Aurora Easton's coffee mug as she set it beside her on the bench in the gazebo. If one could taste the sweetness of fall, it would taste like Mariposa Honey coffee. And the brew was strong enough that Aurora was sure her neighbor and best friend's mom, Lillian Taylor, could smell it in the wind. For the first time in three months, she could sip hot coffee without sweat forming on the back of her neck. She relished in the slight hint of coolness filling the breeze, knowing the summer had finally decided to start its descent. Although Aurora also knew that as soon as she pulled out the blankets, summer would make a sudden return, even if only for a few days. It was the desert's way of reminding everyone to be grateful for giving their air conditioners a well-deserved break.

"Goodbye, summer." She raised her mug in a single cheer to the sky. "And good riddance."

Aurora's girls, Ava and Willa, were still asleep in their beds, and she relished the alone time. Wanting and needing moments to herself caused Aurora to have remorse. Taking a long sip of the rich amber coffee, she hoped it would wash her guilt down with it.

Her gaze attached itself to her home, the only two-story home in all of Woolsey. The sun had faded the pale-yellow siding into an off-white shade. The once bold hunter-green shutters were now a stagnant swamp algae color. Her stacked front patio chairs could use a good scrub to rid the dirt and debris stirred up from the summer's monsoon storms, but if she chased every chore, Aurora would never get a moment's rest.

And this fall was going to be different, it had to be. Aurora couldn't rid her mind of her late husband's constant memory everywhere she looked. Simple things like filling her 4Runner up with gas caused tears to line the bottom lids of her eyes. Mike had always done that for her. And lying alone in bed, listening as the house settled from the heat of the day, vulnerability slid over her as though attached to the sheets she pulled to her chin.

Her mind felt like a broken record these days, rehashing all her memories and future wishes. Aurora watched as a bee buzzed near the lip of her mug and then decided otherwise. The bee reminded her of how much she needed to accomplish with her new career path—she'd surely be buzzing all over the state at some point.

But this would be her second fall without Mike, and she needed to have at least a little break from the daily memories. It was time for her to heal and move on. It didn't do her health any good to drag Mike's memories behind her like an anchor.

She shifted on her tailbone and took another sip from the mug. A slight breeze of cooler air floated past and caused Aurora to close her eyes with gentle delight. It was the final week of October, and the temperature shifted only a week ago. The daytime highs still peaked anywhere between ninety and one hundred, but finally the nights were cooling down to the mid-sixties, allowing Aurora to open the home's windows for the first time since May.

A lizard, about two inches long and concrete in color, skittered up one of the boards supporting the gazebo. While the geckos specifically lived in the front yard, catching bugs on the porch's lights at night, the lizards roamed the backyard.

It had been one of the hottest and driest summers on record for Arizona as a whole, and the opportunity to create something meaningful literally ended up on her property like a ghost. And a small part of her believed Mike had sent it.

During the end of summer, numerous wild horses wandered onto properties all over Woolsey in search of much-needed water and to forage for food. Aurora couldn't understand how everything had come together as she plotted out and dove headfirst into her new venture. It definitely caused second thoughts that miracles do happen. And she'd had no clue she would've ever created a nonprofit organization.

For the last two years, Aurora struggled to find her new place in life, even as a long-term resident of Woolsey. She'd loved being a stay-at-home mom, and was grateful to be able to continue to do so thanks to the life insurance policy, but Aurora needed something more. And she needed something to focus on outside of motherhood, away from the confines of the home, and beyond her comfort zone. And as she took another drink of coffee, she silently scolded herself, once again, for assuming life should be a perfect fairy tale.

Aurora's best friend, Trinity Moore, had stuck to her like glue throughout the first several months after Mike passed. However, Trinity had her hands full with Jolie, teaching, and her side cookie business, leaving her without enough glue to spare. And although Aurora never mentioned it to Trinity, she found it hard to spend time with her and Camden because it only reminded her of the date nights they no longer shared. All Aurora and her girls were now was a three-person third wheel, causing her to wonder if she'd ever fall in love again. More importantly, would she ever be *able* to fall in love? Not only was Woolsey sparse on single men, but she worried no one could ever fill her heart the way Mike had.

Aurora wiped a tear from her left eye and took another sip of coffee as her cell phone vibrated in her pocket. She hoped to hear from a couple of counties, Pima and Pinal, regarding windmill and tank placements. But she expected to hear back from the Arizona Department of Revenue regarding the business, as the state had received her 501(c)(3) nonprofit status from the IRS, and everything else was pretty much a go. Now all Aurora needed was help installing the windmills and adjacent water tanks.

*Sure, there are men in Woolsey.* Aurora sighed a laugh. *But none that would be able or available to help the final part of her business get off the ground, literally.*

"Mommy!" Willa screamed, running out onto the patio from the French doors. "Mommy!"

She waved a hand from the gazebo. "Yes, Willa."

"Mom, you said we could make our big Friday breakfast." Her five-year-old daughter climbed onto her lap and placed her fingers into Aurora's wavy shoulder-length mulberry-colored hair. Willa had her dad's smile and her mom's eyes—thankfully, they went well together.

For the last year, Aurora's change in hair color had been the talk of the town. She used it to express the emotions of losing Mike when she couldn't find a way out of the heartbreak. It was one thing she could control, and she craved and needed it. The first and most significant change was cutting off twelve inches. She followed that up with bleached blonde coloring for six months, then ink black, then she went back to auburn, and for the last three months, it was mulberry. But she and the girls loved the newest color, and it went well with her skin tone.

Aurora kissed Willa's forehead. "I did say we would make a big Friday breakfast, didn't I. Is your sister up yet?"

Willa shook her head no. "She's sleeping like a bear in hubernation."

Aurora laughed and guided her daughter off her lap by holding her hand out. "It's hibernation." Taking her mug in her right hand, she led Willa back toward the house with her left. "Well, I guess Ava will have to wake up and help us."

"I hope she doesn't growl at us." Willa swung her arm with her mom's.

She loved Willa's sense of humor at such a young age and her fascination with animals. Learning about them was educational and a diversion from the memories. Aurora remained astonished by how well the girls had done with the sudden loss of their dad. Not to say they haven't had their ups and downs, but they were far more resilient than she gave them credit for. And Aurora knew that without Ava and Willa, she might not have been able to keep herself from falling into major depression. The girls helped her get out of bed every morning and maintain a schedule that allowed for familiar structure in the home.

As they stepped inside, Aurora's phone buzzed again in her pocket. She'd forgotten to check it a few minutes ago, and after walking through the living room toward the kitchen, Willa let go of her mom's hand and bolted to the pantry, flinging it open. Aurora set her half-full mug of coffee on the edge of the kitchen's island and paused to watch the morning news. A hurricane, Teddy, said to be a Category 3, was upgraded to a 4 within the last twenty-four hours.

"Oh, it's going to hit Louisiana. How horrible."

"Mom!"

When Aurora turned and headed into the kitchen, the gloomy look on her face remained. Willa had managed to dump the entire canister of flour all over the counter and onto the hardwood floor. As Aurora placed her hand across her forehead, the dust from the flour settling filled the air between them.

"Willa, what happened?" She moved closer. "You know you need to wait for help."

"I wanted to do it for you like Daddy did."

She looked around the kitchen at the mess and then back at her daughter. The sudden weight of adult responsibilities pulled down her shoulders but sent a spark to her hands as she scooped up a pile of flour and tossed it in Willa's direction.

"How about we make it better than when Daddy did it?" Aurora picked up another handful and tossed it up in the air.

"Daddy is looking down on us and laughing because this is a mess!" Willa giggled and then leaned over the counter, digging her hands into the pile of flour.

And as the handfuls of flour continued to fill the air, Aurora noticed something more than the feeling of fall—change was afoot, and she smiled at the possibilities.

# Chapter 2

## Gavin

Gavin Hart didn't know if he'd made the right decision. But as he pulled his truck into the driveway of Judge Elizabeth Dunn's house, he somehow managed to crack a smile. He hadn't been back in Woolsey, Arizona in about a year, but it felt good. The dry air seemed to pull his posture straighter and his shoulders back.

His cowboy boots stirred up dust as he walked the dirt path from the truck to the judge's home. Before he could ring the bell, the front door swung open, and the screen door popped forward, causing him to leap backward.

"Gavin, hon." Elizabeth's face warmed with a smile. She stretched out her arms and gave him a good ole warm Southern hug and stepped back, her body holding open the screen door.

"Great to see you, Lizzy."

"Just sorry it's under these circumstances." She crossed her arms. "Well, come on inside, it's still a bit too Arizona–summer out there."

Out of habit, Gavin stomped his boots on the mat before he followed the judge inside, and the cool air-conditioned breeze wrapped around him, causing him to shiver. The house had not changed since his last visit, and he guessed that Mama's room remained the same as well. The soft sounds of Patsy Cline drifted from the television, and two cream candles' flames danced inside the kiva fireplace.

"Do I smell fried chicken?" Gavin leaned toward the scent. "And okra?"

"You just might." Elizabeth headed into the kitchen and motioned for him to follow. "Do you want me to turn the weather on the TV?"

He waved her off as she poured a tall glass of iced tea and handed him the blue-tinted cup. "Unless the hurricane veered off its path, not much sense in findin' out what we already know. Such a shame, I finally finished the renovations on my house, and"—he removed his cowboy hat and pushed his hand through his hair—"I should've known better than to think this wouldn't happen."

Elizabeth flipped the sizzling fried chicken in the pan and picked up a wooden spoon to stir in the tall pot. "Hurricanes happen, and I for one am grateful I don't have to deal with them here. But your poor house . . . everyone's poor homes."

The judge's hair remained the same chili red curly mess he had always known, but he noticed a few more wrinkles lined her forehead, and he knew he too had gained a few gray hairs and wrinkles. Yet, Gavin swore Lizzy must've shrunk a few inches because she was on her tippy-toes stirring the okra at the stove. Although with his six-foot frame, everyone appeared to be short.

"Did you need me to give you a haircut?" Elizabeth pointed in the direction of his head.

"Once a babysitter, always a babysitter. Although I don't think babysitters are supposed to be barbers."

"Locks of Love would gladly accept your donation."

"It's not that long." He pretended to itch a spot near his ear, realizing that maybe it had grown a bit *too* long. In a week, he might have to tuck it behind his ears. As a single man, there was no one to point out when he should trim his hair or care that he hadn't shaved his face.

Gavin leaned back in the chair and took a long sip of tea, and the ice bumped against his upper lip. "Thanks for having me. I feel awful for imposin', but with the hotels in the borderin' states all booked, I didn't feel like sittin' in all the traffic to head farther north." Of course, Gavin could've traveled anywhere to escape, but nothing beat spending time with Lizzy and relaxing in the town of Woolsey. It was almost as if he were back home.

"Oh, hush. It's the best time of the year to be here. Fall is a delight, and in the final days of summer, when you can feel the switch battlin' it out in the air, I think the screams of delight that the heat is on its way out can be heard in the wind."

"It's a dry heat here." Gavin's eyes traveled to the photo of a young Mama on the kitchen wall opposite the stove. "That's what I always hear."

Elizabeth pulled two plates from the cupboard. "Gosh, don't say that around Woolsey. The last thing the town folks want to hear is *that* worn-out phrase."

"But it's true."

The judge smirked. "Of course it is."

"Either way, I'll be careful when I'm out and about." Gavin's mouth watered at the smells of home hanging in the air. "Can I be of any help?"

"I could use some muscle to move some heavier boxes out to the garage, but otherwise, not much to do. Mama's old room is all ready for you." Elizabeth tapped a spoon of okra, piled high onto Gavin's plate, added two pieces of greasy fried chicken, and brought it to the table.

"Are you sure it's okay I stay here?" Gavin sat up straight in his chair and continued to balance his tan cowboy hat on his right knee.

"Even if I said no, which I wouldn't, Woolsey doesn't have a motel, so no, of course, I don't mind." Elizabeth joined him at the table, and before she could place her napkin in her lap, he'd already picked up his chicken, the grease soaking into his fingertips. "How bad do you think it'll be?"

He didn't need to ask what she was referring to: Teddy, Category 4 Teddy. "With a name like Teddy, you'd think it would be a big hug-filled Category 1. But we know it'll be as bad as they say. It always is; last time, I was stupid enough to assume stayin' would be a safer bet than fleein'." Gavin stabbed his fork into a piece of okra.

"Was that a Category 2?"

Gavin nodded and swallowed. "Lorenzo, yeah, he was a Cat 2. Not too bad for one with a much more powerful name. I expected Lorenzo to do a lot more damage. But Teddy, well, I anticipate the power to be out for at least a week. And who knows how long the water will be off for. Being so far from services and what they're predictin', as far as the surge, the water levels could take weeks to recede."

"Maybe look at this as a vacation, although forced and stress-ridden." Elizabeth wiped her mouth with her napkin.

"I plan to put myself to good use while I'm here. You know I'm not one to sit around." He nibbled the remaining chicken and picked up his second crispy piece. "How is . . . the woman who lost her husband, starts with an A. She's Trinity's best friend."

"Aurora. She's been doin' well as far as I know. But she's been so busy with her little girls, tryin' to make sure they remain as unfazed as possible. She sold her plane, so the buzzin' over town in her crop duster has stopped drivin' us all batty. *That's* been nice—not to have to deal with the little earthquakes anymore—my dishes appreciate it."

Gavin chuckled. "I remember meeting her. Twice I think. She seems like a fun person, such a shame she had to adapt to suddenly single parentin'."

"That reminds me, I made a hummingbird cake, well, cupcakes. Aurora's girls love them. Maybe you could drop some of them off for me?"

Gavin set his fork down. "Oh, no, no, Lizzy. I'm not stayin'. My home is in Louisiana."

"I'm only askin' you to drop off some cupcakes, not date her. Plus, she could use your help."

"I'm sure she doesn't want a visit from a strange man. It's only been, what, a year since she lost her husband?"

Elizabeth shook her head. "No, it's goin' on two years now."

*Had time gone by that fast lately?* It seemed that he was in Trinity and Camden's living room only months ago. He tried to recall what Aurora looked like, but nothing came to mind, only that he knew her name and hoped he would recognize her if he spotted her in town.

Gavin wiped his mouth with the napkin and tucked it under his plate. "Why can't you just go over and drop off the cupcakes for Aurora?"

"First of all, Aurora can't have any, she's allergic to eggs, they're for the girls. And second, I would never tell you what to do, only offer a suggestion or two."

Gavin leaned over his plate. "I suggest you let me try one of those hummingbird cupcakes and don't meddle in my love life."

"I can't meddle in a love life that doesn't exist. I'm a judge, not a magician." Elizabeth crossed her arms over her chest.

With the chicken held up in front of his lips, Gavin prevented her from seeing his mouth turn up into a grin.

# Chapter 3

## Aurora

One of Aurora's most challenging tasks was trying to grocery shop with her two little girls in tow. It took twice as long and cost twice as much. And with Halloween right around the corner, she was sure she'd have to face the candy bag battle. At least it was October, and she didn't have to risk getting sunburned walking the fifty feet from her 4Runner to the front door of the Shop and Save.

Taking Willa's hand in her right and Ava's in her left, they made their way across the packed dirt parking lot. Aurora's stomach groaned as her flip-flops met the worn wooden decking of the grocery store's patio. Lunch—she'd fed the girls, but had become sidetracked trying to get out the door, thus leaving her sandwich, untouched, on the kitchen's island. And since it wasn't Saturday, Charlie Tow didn't have the barbecue going.

Aurora's sundress, adorned with tiny yellow flowers, fluttered against her knees as the front door swung open and Ezra Hackenberg exited, balancing a paper bag in the crook of his arm.

"Aurora! Girls!" Ezra stepped aside, holding the door open.

"Thank you, good to see you, too. How are Wyatt and the kids doing?" Aurora let go of the girls' hands, allowing them to file into the store one at a time.

"They're doing well, Jeter and Jasmine are back home with Wyatt watching a movie." Ezra motioned to the bag by raising it a few inches. "I was sent on a snack run."

"How nice of you." Aurora felt a forced smile crease her lips. Mike had always made snack runs for them.

Ezra reached his hand out and set it on Aurora's wrist for half a second. "*Really* great to see *you*."

She looked forward to the day when residents didn't tilt their heads and say *great to see you*. Like her leaving the house was some sort of miracle.

"Enjoy your movie." Aurora spun around and grabbed a shopping cart.

They made their way down the first aisle with her daughters on opposite sides of the cart. Ava had the task of holding the shopping list and was the only reason why it wasn't left back home on the kitchen counter. Willa was in charge of pointing out everything she wanted that wasn't on the list.

As Aurora turned down another aisle, Ava hung onto her mom's arm, and Willa skipped near her side as she loaded up on a week's worth of groceries.

"Mom, can we get some candy?" Ava asked.

"They don't have any."

"Mom, that's not the truth. They have Halloween candy. Jared at school said so," Ava asserted.

A male voice under a tan cowboy hat said, "I heard candy keeps the monsters under your bed away."

Aurora tilted her head in the direction of the cowboy holding a bag of candy corn. "Why, that's ridiculous . . . wait, Gavin?"

"Aurora?" His eyes squinted and opened wider. "Your hair is a different color."

She had only met him twice, once at Mama's funeral and last Christmas at the library's annual party. She remembered his accent and cowboy hat. And judging by the worn fabric, it was probably the same one he wore now.

Aurora's hands squeezed the cart's handle as a wave of warmth traveled up the front of her neck. "Yes, I wanted to do something bold." She touched a strand of hair.

"I think the color looks great on you."

"Thank you." She twisted a finger around a piece. "Wonderful to see you again. I didn't know you were in town. When did you get in?"

"Yesterday evening. A last-minute travel emergency." Gavin tipped up his hat with his hand, showing off his chocolate-brown eyes.

"Oh no, that's right, the hurricane." Aurora's hand left the cart and rested against her chest. "Gosh, I saw it on the news. Should you be so far from home?"

Gavin snatched a second bag of candy corn off the shelf and dropped it into his basket. "It's a mess all over the state. Stayin' wouldn't have done me any good."

"Mom, can we get candy like him?" Ava pointed at Gavin.

Aurora glanced at the bags of candy corn in his basket. "No, honey, that candy is gross."

Gavin's eyes narrowed, and his lips parted into a gasp. "Candy corn is the best fall candy around, maybe even beatin' out all other candy."

She couldn't help but chuckle. "No, candy corn is like a bloody Halloween costume. Not everyone likes it."

"Did you just compare candy corn to a bloody costume?"

Aurora's cheeks flushed, and she pressed her lips together. "It's the truth." And the truth was also that her heartbeat was thumping loud enough she could hear it in her ears. *Gosh, he's attractive, especially when he smiles.*

Gavin raised an eye. "That statement is as true as sayin' hot butter won't slip off the cob."

Her cheeks continued to warm, and she glanced down at the ground in hopes of refocusing her thoughts.

"I'm surprised to see anything fall here. I mean, fall and Arizona don't seem likely to mix." Gavin tossed one of the bags in the air and caught it. "Maybe if they make candy corn into a freezer pop?"

Willa attempted to twirl while holding onto her mom's hand. "Arizona has a lot to offer, especially in the fall, if you know where to look. How long will you be in town?"

"I have no idea. It depends on the after-effects of the storm." He glanced at the girls and then returned eye contact with Aurora. "How have you been?"

She instinctively took a deep breath and held it, wondering if he wanted the truth or a lie. Most people wanted something in between, something which gave them a bit of gossip but not enough information to feel bad for the other person.

"Lizzy mentioned you started a nonprofit?"

*Thank goodness he changed the subject!* Aurora tucked her hair behind her right ear. "Yes, but I'm at the point where I need some assistance, physical work."

"Anything I could help with? I would love to be of use, if possible."

The last thing Aurora wanted was to be needy, but it was a business, not charity. As an outsider, Gavin could be the perfect pity-free help she needed.

Her left arm suddenly dipped, nearly pulling her to the floor. "Ouch, Willa." She snapped back upright.

"Sorry, Mommy." Willa wrapped her arms around Aurora's waist.

15

"Are you alright?" Gavin's hand outstretched in Aurora's direction.

Aurora focused on his hand as he drew it back toward his hip. She allowed her breath to release, but it didn't help her heartbeat slow down.

"Oh yes, I'm a mom. We can withstand more than a bull rider, and we have better outfits."

Gavin chuckled hard enough that his eyes squinted.

Aurora smiled. "Actually, from what I remember, you work in construction."

"True." He adjusted his cowboy hat.

Willa reached her arms up to Aurora, who picked her up and rested her youngest daughter on her hip.

"Are you sure you need my help?" Gavin's eyes gave her a once-over. "You're a lot stronger than you look."

"I'm going to take that as a compliment." She felt Ava's hand on her back.

"As you should." He switched the basket from his right hand to his left, and she peeked at it—other than Halloween candy, there was a circle of Camembert cheese and a loaf of French bread.

"Then, thank you." Aurora giggled like she was twenty again and covered her mouth.

Ava moved towards Gavin, and he lowered to her level, shoving his hand forward. "I'm Gavin. Who are you?"

Ava took his hand and shook it with vigor. "Nice to meet you, Gavin. I'm Ava Easton. I'm the old one."

Gavin laughed. "Is it fun to be the oldest one?"

Ava put a hand on her hip. "Usually."

Gavin chuckled as he stood back up. "That reminds me, Lizzy said she had some hummingbird cupcakes for the girls. I can drop them off later today if that works for you?"

"Mom, say yes." Willa yanked on her mom's shirt. "I love hummingbird cupcakes."

"What my girls always need more of—sugar." Aurora rested her hand on the top of Ava's head.

Gavin grinned. "If you want, we can talk about how I can help you out with your nonprofit."

"You know, that sounds great, thank you." Aurora set Willa on the floor.

"Shall we say four o'clock?"

"We shall." Aurora put both hands onto the cart. "And if certain sugary items happen to be forgotten, that's okay too. Elizabeth is like a grandma that gets the grandkids hyper and then drops them off for the parent to deal with."

"She does have her good qualities." Gavin tossed a bag of caramel apple suckers on top of the candy corn. "I'll let you get back to shoppin'. It was better than candy corn runnin' into you."

Why did she keep blushing when he said certain things? Aurora nodded. "See you at four."

He touched the brim of his hat and gave a single nod as the girls waved bye. Aurora pushed the shopping cart down the aisle and scolded herself for thinking how handsome the man in the cowboy hat was.

# Chapter 4

## Gavin

Later the same day, Gavin adjusted his cowboy hat before knocking on Aurora's front door. He'd contemplated not wearing it since they'd be inside, but he felt naked without it.

His palms began to sweat against the container of cupcakes and moths fluttered in his stomach. Seeing Aurora in the grocery store only made him feel ridiculous that he could've forgotten how beautiful she was and silly that he ever questioned whether he'd recognize her. Having the last several hours to think about seeing her again only caused him to be nervous.

The front door swung open, and the screen door shaded Aurora. He stepped back a foot, and she pushed the screen forward. A floral dress hung just above her knees, and her feet were bare except for the rich merlot nail polish on her toes.

"Dang, you didn't lose the cupcakes." She stood aside and rested herself up against the door. Her hair looked nearly purple in the sunlight that filtered inside the home, causing a spark of curiosity about getting to know Aurora better. She motioned for him to come inside.

"Sorry," he raised the container in the air, "besides, a little sugar isn't a bad thing."

In front of him, past the wooden staircase, a vast hall led to the back of the house. Immediately to his left was a study, and to his right, a family room. It reminded him of a classic Southern Colonial-style house he would find back home. He'd remodeled or restored countless Colonials over the years and was fond of the layout. It was the perfect family home but not ideal for a single person due to the amount of square footage to manage.

Gavin handed the Tupperware of cupcakes to Aurora. She took it and peered over her shoulder up the staircase. Then placing her finger to her lip, "Shhh, maybe we can sneak in some non-kid time before they realize you're here and there are cupcakes."

He followed her down the hall, hearing some thumping coming from upstairs towards the back of the house. French doors looked out into the backyard, and to his left a living room, to his right the kitchen. The walls and décor were different shades of light blues and rustic whites, which he found calming and presented an atmosphere that nearly felt like home.

"The girls are upstairs, and against my better judgment, I put a movie on for them in my bedroom. I love them, but having a break is nice, too."

Aurora popped open the lid to the container and pulled a hummingbird cupcake from it. She held it up to her nose. "Smells so yummy." Taking her finger, she swiped a line of frosting off the top. "Thankfully, I can have the frosting. The girls won't miss one cupcake. I'm so sorry. I have the worst manners." Aurora lifted two small plates out of a nearby cupboard and set one in front of him and one for her. "Can I get you something to drink?"

"Whatever you're havin'."

"I like the way you think." Aurora moved to the refrigerator and grabbed a bottle of half-empty wine from the door, flashing him the label like Vanna White—pinot gris.

Gavin watched as she set two wineglasses in front of their plates and poured a little bit of crisp-looking liquid into each one.

"I know this sounds bad, but I miss drinking with someone."

"What about Trinity? Do you still spend time together?"

"We don't see each other as much as we used to, especially with Jolie taking up a lot of her time on top of her cookie business and being a teacher." Aurora wrapped her hand around the wine bottle. "I mean, we see each other around town, and Camden helps out so we can have girl time every once in a while, but regular hang outs are few and far between now."

He didn't want to ask, and he didn't need to. Aurora missed her husband. They must have enjoyed many long nights chatting, watching movies, and going on adventures. Just the thought of sitting next to Aurora on a porch swing, admiring the night sky, and enjoying a glass of wine caused his heartbeat to speed up.

"While I'm in town, if you'd like, I'll be your wine buddy." Gavin held his glass up, and Aurora met it with a slight *clink*.

"Deal." Aurora leaned over the counter and took another finger of frosting off the cupcake. A little white frosting stuck to the tip of her lip, and she wiped it away with her tongue. Aurora's free-spirited personality drew Gavin in. Between bites of his cupcake, he had to remind himself that he wasn't staying, and Aurora had her own life and was probably not even close to being ready to date.

"Elizabeth makes some of the most delicious dishes; it puts my cooking to shame. At least the ones I can eat."

"I doubt that." Gavin wiped the cream cheese frosting from his lips with his thumb and checked his goatee for any he might have missed. "But havin' an egg allergy must be a real bummer."

She held up the uneaten cupcake in her hand. "Thankfully, there are substitutes on the market now, but it was rough as a child."

Gavin cleared his throat and reminded himself to find some egg-free recipes. Maybe he could cook for her. He *wanted* to cook for her. He didn't even want to cook for himself. "Now tell me, what can I do to help you?"

"The business—I'm starting locally before I decide how to move throughout the rest of the state. I'm slated to build at least three windmills in Woolsey to pull water from underground. I have the windmill kits, lines, and containers for storage, but none of them are assembled yet."

"I can help you with all of that, no problem." Gavin peeled off the rest of the cupcake's wrapper. "What got you started on this nonprofit rescue?"

"After Mike died, I struggled to focus on anything. I was a stay-at-home mom, and even with putting all my energy into the girls, it never felt like enough. They're both in school for full days now. Without having Mike to at least speak with on the phone between his meetings, it was hard to not feel lonely and, dare I say, unimportant. The company he owned was something I didn't want to take on, and he traveled at least one week out of the month. Not that I could leave my girls to travel for work even if I desired to, so his two partners bought my share. For me, I needed to do something meaningful. Something my girls would be proud of and that would push me forward into a sort of return to the work field. Unfortunately, at this point, I feel that they might be picking up on my depressive state."

"I'm sure your girls know you're doing your best. But I do think this organization you created sounds honorable. How did you decide on the rescue platform?" He popped the final bite of the cupcake into his mouth.

"The idea literally came right in front of me." Aurora smiled, and Gavin found himself staring into her eyes. But not any stare—he was trying to find some sort of history behind them, craving to learn all he could. He watched how her eyes reflected the light around the room, making them sparkle brightly.

"A wild horse wandered onto the property and was trying to get water from the sprinkler I had going for the girls. I don't think he would have come around if he wasn't desperate for a drink because they rarely want anything to do with people. Let alone little kids."

Gavin washed down the last bite of the cupcake with a sip of wine and held the glass in his hand. "I can attest that havin' the horse do somethin' such as that was indeed a sign."

She licked the rest of the frosting off her finger. "Are you sure you're okay to help me with the windmills and basins? It's a lot of work, as you can imagine, and the weather is still rather warm."

"It's quite odd, but I feel like new life has been breathed into me without the humidity drippin' off my bones. I'm more than willin' to assist. I find helpin' animals to be one of the best and most worthy causes. However, I get the notion that you need a lot more help from me than you're lettin' on. Is there anything else I can assist you with here?" He glanced around the kitchen but didn't see anything that stood out to him as needing fixing.

Aurora brought her finger to her bottom lip and pinched it as though doing so would keep whatever she wanted to say at bay. "How much do you charge for something like this?"

"I should be payin' you. I honestly don't know what else I could be doin' with my time, and the last thing I need is to be sittin' around, starin' at the ceiling tryin' to figure out what stage of disaster my house is in back in Jesser."

"How long do you plan on staying in Woolsey?" Aurora snatched the wine bottle and equally emptied the remaining liquid into their glasses.

She tilted her head, making sure she matched them was like watching a little kid measure out a bowl of ice cream. *How is everything Aurora does cute?*

"To be honest, I don't know." Gavin rested his elbows on the island and set his hand on the stem of the wineglass. "If I had stayed back home, there would've been nothin' I could've done. Sure, I can help with cleanup around Jesser, but it often leads to more dangerous situations. I already let the sheriff's office know I was out of town and that no animals were at the house. That'll free up their services to help others who were not able to leave or didn't want to for one reason or another."

"I couldn't imagine living someplace where I had to worry about losing my house. It's such a catastrophic thought." Aurora leaned forward on the island and gazed into his eyes.

Gavin had no idea how it was possible to feel such comfort being around someone he barely knew, in a home he'd never been in before, and the notion frightened him. This was not the time or place for feelings. He adjusted his hat, hesitant to take it off. "So, nothin' much in the way of weather happens here in Arizona?"

"Not really." Aurora eased up and took a sip of wine. "I mean, we do get a few earthquakes—maybe one every five years. There are flash floods from the monsoons, but overall, nothing like hurricanes and tornadoes. Monsoons bring strong winds, which causes an insane amount of dust. It's like trying to see through a blizzard, but it doesn't smell as pleasant."

He chuckled and took a sip of freshly poured wine.

23

"Honestly in all my years, other than dust getting in every crack and crevice and trees blown over, it's a pretty natural-disaster-free life. I mean, if you're caught out in it, you have to stop driving and pull over, but I'm sure you have to do that with tornadoes. And you can't out-drive a hurricane."

"I remember seeing a few amazing pictures on the national news about your dust storms. They engulf the entire landscape, an avalanche of dirt rolling over the tops of buildings and houses."

"Oh yes, it's quite a sight to see it coming in from afar."

He suddenly had a desire to see this wall of dust up close. Lungs be damned. "From what I've seen, there's not a lot of . . . history here, from an architectural standpoint." Gavin glimpsed around the kitchen, trying to observe what he could without it looking obvious that he was scoping out what life was like for Aurora and her girls. His aspiration to learn more about them simultaneously thrilled and worried him.

Aurora nodded. "Yes, and no. I think Sun City has some classic '60s and '70s-era style homes, even though they're only about fifty years old. But you know, down south, Bisbee was founded in, I believe, the late 1800s and has some pretty cool buildings. Just not the same as what you would find in your neck of the woods or on the East Coast."

"Your house here is a Southern Colonial style home. It's very unusual to find this type of home in the desert Southwest."

"That's probably one of the reasons why I love it so much." Aurora sighed as she gazed out the window above the kitchen sink.

"From what I know so far, the house suits you." Gavin made eye contact with Aurora, and it felt like shock waves fused their vision together. "The little I know." His palms instantly warmed. *Stop it!* Gavin rubbed his hands along the top of his knees. "There are some amazing creole cottages and double-gallery houses all over Jesser from the 1800s. There are spirits and memories in the South that suck you in."

"Dare I admit I've never been to Louisiana?" Aurora crossed her arms.

"Never? Then you must come for a visit. Your girls would love it."

When she smiled and tilted her head down, he swore he caught her blushing. "We would like that, as long as you could show us around, of course."

"It would be my pleasure." Gavin swallowed, and it felt as though he were trying to keep his heart from bursting up through his throat. "So, there must be a story behind this house."

"There is, because you're correct, it's not the typical desert architecture for a reason. My grandpa and his brother built this house for his wife, my grandma. And my grandma was from a small town in Georgia, and in order for him to convince her to come out here to the dusty desert, he had to give her the best gift possible. He had to give her . . . home."

"Do you mean to tell me you have Southern roots?"

"I do," Aurora drawled like a Southern belle. She curtsied, grabbing the edge of her skirt as though it had a crinoline under it.

If Gavin hadn't been sitting down already, his legs would've easily wobbled from his admiration for Aurora.

"See, my grandparents met right before the Vietnam War. My grandpa was from Phoenix, and he was drafted and stationed at Fort Stewart Army Base in Georgia. My grandma worked as a waitress at a diner where my grandpa ate a few extra meals when he first relocated there. Long story short, they met at the diner, and she waited for him to return from the war. And when he did, she'd just lost both her parents in a car accident. My grandma was hesitant to move so far away from the only life she'd ever known, but when he agreed to build her a house that would remind her of home, she said yes."

"Then, this is your family's home?" He pushed all five fingers of his left hand onto the island's top.

"Yes, my grandparents lived here until they passed away. My parents inherited the house and raised me here. My grandparents had only one son, my father. He kept the house when he married my mom."

"How did you end up with the house now, if you don't mind me askin'?"

"You know those retro houses out in Sun City?"

"They didn't!" Gavin leaned back and chuckled.

"They did. My dad is a golf fanatic, and my mom has all of these women's clubs. I mean every club—book club, bridge club, sewing club, and there's probably even a high tea club. Sun City is a great community, and for them, it works well. I think that my father wasn't the country, back roads kind of guy his parents wanted him to be."

"You seem very comfortable here."

Aurora took a deep breath, her chest rising in effect as she stared at the walls around her. "This is my heaven on earth, even on the hottest days. I hope that at least one of my girls wants to keep the house and raise her family here, but if not, that's okay, too."

"You don't want to grow old in this house?"

Aurora sipped her wine and turned around; her gaze remained at the window over the kitchen sink. "I would, but it's a lot to keep up for one person."

Gavin wanted to comment yet held his tongue. Aurora would for sure remarry someday; she was too perfect not to.

# Chapter 5

## Aurora

Aurora lifted an azure blue casserole dish over her girls' heads and set it in the middle of the kitchen table.

"Are you sure you don't mind me stayin' for dinner?" Gavin grabbed the napkin off the table and draped it across his lap.

"We don't mind," Willa said, using two hands to pick up her glass of water before taking a sip.

"Thank you, sweetie, for using both hands, and Willa is correct—we don't mind. I appreciate the adult company. Besides, my girls and I always have leftovers that we never get around to until it's too late."

"They're green!" Willa chimed.

"It's called mold, Willa," Ava instructed.

She handed Gavin a serving spoon and watched as he scooped a non-spicy enchilada out of the dish, the steam rising off it. As she lowered herself into her chair, multiple thoughts raced through her mind. Not only was Gavin a kind man, but she found him attractive, and there was a sense of comfort being around him. However, beyond that, simply having a man at the table again felt both welcoming and out of place.

"I hope you like it. The girls don't like spicy foods, and we live in Arizona. Go figure. But after six months of working on this recipe, I finally perfected it, and thankfully, they love it."

"Can one have an enchilada if it's not spicy?" Gavin handed the serving spoon back to Aurora.

"I guess you'll find out." Aurora half-smiled as she scooped a little onto Willa's plate and then Ava's plate before setting the dish next to her. "Of course, it goes best with a little sour cream."

After Aurora had loaded up her plate, she glanced around and noticed the girls had already started to eat but not Gavin. He stared right at her, and she tried not to blush at the nervousness of butterflies he caused.

"Oh, don't wait for me, Gavin, go on and eat." Aurora waved her clean fork at him.

"My mama raised me better than that." He gripped his fork and then brought it to his plate.

Aurora focused on the meal in front of her and took a bite. When she looked up, Gavin had a forkful of enchilada, and he winked before bringing it to his mouth.

She held her breath, waiting for his reaction.

He lowered his fork onto his plate and leaned back in the chair. "Okay, this is delicious."

"Thank you." She tried not to let Gavin see her sigh with relief.

Aurora wasn't only happy that he liked it but also having him there allowed her shoulders to relax for the first time in . . . she couldn't recall how long. Or at least she noticed that her shoulders weren't raised high enough to cover her ears. Dare she admit she felt secure and safe with a man she knew very little about? Not that anything bad happened in Woolsey. Since her senior year in high school, she'd taken self-defense classes and a yearly refresher to brush up on her skills. She'd spent many days and nights alone with the girls while Mike traveled for work, but she truly missed the protection of a man.

Heat traveled up Aurora's neck as she sensed Gavin's eyes on her. She couldn't remember the last time a man paid attention to her—and not just a glance but with contemplating depth. Yet, at the same time as feeling admired, she also became uneasy. There shouldn't be another man, especially one in the house that she and Mike had shared while raising their girls.

"Okay, I'm sold." Gavin's smooth Southern accent eased over the table. "Non-spicy enchiladas are amazin'."

At least now it looked like Aurora was simply embarrassed by his kind words for her cooking and not the intensity of his admiring stare. "Thank you."

"Gavin?" Willa asked, holding her fork in her fist. "What are your in-ten-sons?"

All the blood in Aurora's body suddenly shot to the tip of her nose and ears as she covered her face and mumbled through her fingers, "Willa, where did you learn that word?"

"My intentions, Willa," Gavin said, resting his palm on top of his opposite hand without a hint of embarrassment, "is to help your mom out with her new company."

Willa closed her eyes and nodded her head. "Okay." She slumped forward. "But can we do something fun, too?"

Aurora knew she and Gavin were the equivalent of fish in a shark-filled tank. Allowing her eyes to grow wide open, she warned him of the danger they were in. Gavin raised his wineglass to cover his face as though it would protect him, but she could see his smile through the pinot gris.

"What do you have in mind, Willa?" Gavin inquired.

She wiggled in her seat. "On TV, they said a buckle list is fun. A fall one. I want to do a fall buckle list."

First, Aurora made a mental note to do a better job of monitoring what Willa was watching, and second, she said, "I think you mean buck*et* list."

"Can we do it?" Willa had a smudge of sour cream on the top of her lip. "A buck-et list?"

"Of course we may." Aurora picked up her wineglass.

Gavin set his fork down. "Wait a minute, there can't possibly be anything fall-related to do here in Arizona."

"That sounds like a challenge to me. A challenge that we need to prove Gavin wrong about, right girls?"

The girls both nodded their heads yes.

"I guess I have a lot to learn about Arizona." He smiled softly at her.

After they finished dinner, Gavin helped Aurora clear the dinner table, and the girls headed into the living room off the open kitchen. They removed several children's books off the nearby bookcase and carried them to the couch.

Gavin set the stack of four plates on the counter next to the sink. "They enjoy readin'?"

"Oh yes, it's our routine after dinner. First, the girls sit and read while I clean up the kitchen. Then when I'm done, we reread the books together."

Aurora set the empty casserole dish in the kitchen sink and added soap. "You honestly don't have to do the bucket list with us," she whispered, taking a glance at the couch. "I'm sorry she sprang that on you."

Gavin peered over at the girls and then back at Aurora. His closeness to her caused goose bumps to form on the tops of her arms. The scent of amber and hickory radiated from him, and she placed her hands on the edge of the sink and tried to focus on anything *but* Gavin.

He crossed his arms over his chest and leaned back on the counter. "I can't think of the last time I was excited about anything havin' to do with autumn."

"I'm excited, too." Aurora's stomach fluttered with anticipation while hope and happiness coursed through her. Yet, at that moment, she only wanted one thing, regardless of where it came from — she never wanted the feeling of happiness to disappear.

# Chapter 6

## Gavin

After returning from Aurora's house, Gavin paced the floor in the tiny guest bedroom. In the background, an old-school thirty-two-inch television reported the latest update of the Category 4 hurricane having made landfall and Teddy working its way north, straight towards Jesser Parish. But instead of worrying about his house back home, as he should be, he fretted about his instant feelings for Aurora.

Sure, they weren't strangers, but their paths crossing in the past were nothing intimate like the supper they'd shared tonight. And now that Aurora was widowed, it changed everything and made it more difficult than simply being single. There was a degree of emotion and feelings that went with being a widow. Thinking about it caused a certain amount of guilt, and he flopped onto the edge of the bed, burying his head in his hands. But on the other hand, spending time with Aurora and her girls had caused him to immediately feel at home, as though they were longtime friends catching up on all the latest in life.

A gentle rap came at his door, and he got up to open it.

"I thought you might like this." Lizzy stood in the hall, holding two mason jars with what looked like cloudy water with greenery floating in them. However, he knew it was much more potent.

"Perfect." He took the mint julep and enjoyed a long sip before returning to the edge of the bed. Sinking into the mattress, he sighed, lowering his shoulders.

The judge leaned against the doorframe, crossed her arms, and raised the drink to her lips. "Her girls are exuberant."

"They definitely take after their mom, mini versions of Aurora." Gavin allowed the alcohol to take hold and loosen the rigidness in his arms. "The girls suggested we make a fall bucket list. It was cute; Willa called it a buck*le* list. I guess there are fall things to do here, which seems unlikely."

"So I've heard, though I haven't done much travelin' around the state. I always find myself in town or in another state. But a fall bucket list, that would be fun. Aurora knows so much about Arizona and things to do. I'm still learning. And you'll be here for Halloween, I'm sure she'll drag you to Jennifer and Greg's haunted house party. They throw it every year. The entire town shows up—kids and adults. I went for the first time last year and had a blast. But you have to wear a costume."

"I'll go as a cowboy." He crossed his feet at his ankles.

"It's not considered a costume if you always wear it."

"What did you dress up as last year?"

"That's not the point." She took a quick drink.

"Let me guess, a judge." Gavin chuckled. "No more about me. What's going on in your life? There are some nice hydrangeas out there in a vase."

Elizabeth puffed up the curls on the right side of her hair with her free hand. "It's nothing. I mean R. J., over at the hardware store, sent them after our date. He was only bein' nice."

"So, you're dating him?"

"No, he's clearly in love with Lillian."

"Then why did he send you flowers?"

"We should be talking about you, not my lack of a love life, or messed up one. But to be fair, there are only three bachelors in this town, and two of them love Lillian, and I've been here long enough for those men to make a move."

"Well, who's number three?" Gavin moved the drink to his other hand.

"William Adams, the courthouse guard. But he's a wee bit older than me."

"Maybe his front-wheeled walker is getting stuck on his way over."

Elizabeth covered her mouth, and her eyes pinched close. "That's funny and also not appropriate. I'm no spring chicken. William isn't *that* old, just older than someone I would be compatible with. Say, have you heard from anyone back home yet?"

Gavin turned to the television. "I tried to get ahold of Jeanna Ray, but nothing. There must be major power outages because she nor her husband answered their home phone, and neither of them remembers to charge their cell phone. I left them a message on both. Have you spoken with anyone?"

"I called to check on Magnolia, and she said they were up in Shreveport and had no clue as to the state of their house. I know they didn't want to go too far with Barbara bein' in the nursin' home."

"That's as good as anyone can do, I suppose." He shrugged his shoulders and readjusted himself on the edge of the bed. "I called my pa, but you know him. No time to talk, stubborn as always, probably checkin' on all the people in town."

"That man never rests."

Gavin's papa moved to Ruston back when his parents divorced. His mama was living her own life, doing whatever she wanted out in Lexington. Besides a few phone calls for birthdays and holidays, Gavin didn't have much contact with her anymore. The entire situation, when he thought about it, hurt. He missed his parents, especially his mother. However, nothing had changed since he was a kid. It wasn't until he became an adult that he realized the dynamics of why they split up and why they would never get back together. And unfortunately, why he'd never have the relationship he wanted with his mother.

"You were right about Willa and Ava. They seem to be doin' well, but Aurora gave off this vibe of bein', well to be honest . . . lonely." Gavin stretched his legs out.

"I think she's been considerably focused on the girls—making sure they continue to thrive in life and keepin' things as normal as she can—that she forgot about her own happiness."

"Hopefully, as she moves further into runnin' her nonprofit, it will help distract her a bit more from the past. And this fall bucket list—I'm excited to see what's in store. But I hope I'm not oversteppin' in their lives."

"I doubt that's possible. Besides, Aurora needs your help. You're the most capable of assistin' her with those windmills. Just don't go fallin' in love. You don't live here."

He *needed* the reminder because telling himself that wasn't working.

# Chapter 7

## Aurora

"There was a huge price difference between the six-foot and eight-foot steel windmill towers." Aurora stood in front of the pieces laid about, just outside the north side of her two hundred acres. "And this spot is constantly windy, so I didn't feel the height difference would matter much."

Gavin nodded but didn't say anything. Instead, he continued to run his hand back and forth against the side rim of his cowboy hat. He looked as though he'd just stepped off the *Open Range* movie set with the way his boots peeked out perfectly from under his well-worn jeans, and an oversized army-green button-down shirt protected his muscles from the harsh desert sun.

"You won't get too hot in those long sleeves, will you?"

Gavin craned his neck down. "I might, but I'll take that over a sunburn. The sunshine is intense here, as though it's aimin' to penetrate the bone."

"I would say the same thing about the humidity of the South."

"You're right about that." Gavin flashed a grin, and she felt the reaction of delight reach her bones too. "The air hangs off you like Spanish moss."

In front of them was the entire contents for one of the three windmills Aurora had purchased—the vane, motor, stub tower, and brake kit. She prayed she hadn't missed anything. She'd been able to haul the parts on the flatbed hitched to her ATV out to the build site and would hate if anything had been forgotten back at the house.

"The galvanized metal tanks will be here in two days. I'm hoping by sinking them into the land about two feet or so it will help keep it more stable, but not too low that cows are using it to bathe in."

"I believe you know more than I do about windmills." Gavin rested his hands on his hips.

"I've probably studied this more than I ever studied anything in college." Aurora yanked her baseball cap tighter down over her hair. The sun wasn't directly overhead yet, and she was already tired of squinting even with her sunglasses on. "The well driller came out about three weeks ago, and I got lucky. The three spots I planned for placement were predicted as good for the windmills. He hit the water at about 280 feet here, then 290 at the west end, and the other spot was about 300 feet. After he drilled, cased, and capped them with a well seal, I had the size windmills that I'd need and ordered them."

"Speedy shipping. Some things astonish me." Gavin crossed his arms over his chest.

"It's hard to amaze me when Willa thinks of things like wanting to have socks that aren't inside out or right side up."

Gavin glanced down at the ground and back up at Aurora, giving her a puzzled look.

"When she was younger, she used to get frustrated with putting on her socks. The heel always ended up on top of her foot, or if she got it on correctly, it was inside out."

"Let me guess, you made her turn it right side in?"

Aurora's mouth parted in question. "Of course. Why do you wear your socks inside out on purpose?"

"Not on purpose, but it's a sock. No one knows it's on inside out." Gavin sneered.

"Well, now I know what's going on inside your boots." Aurora tilted her head and gave a knowing smile.

Gavin stepped forward. "Or do you?" He winked, and all the heat in her body shot to her cheeks as she blinked firmly several times to try and rid the romantic thoughts gaining speed through her mind. "With instructions, it should be pretty straightforward." Gavin kicked up dust when he walked around the parts. "I watched a few videos online last night since I've never put one of these together before. From what I gathered, it seems like we build everythin' layin' it out on the ground, and then the hard part will be raisin' them to meet in the middle."

Aurora stretched her arms in front of her. "I guess it's best to dive right in." She pulled the folded-up directions from her back jeans pocket.

Gavin stepped up behind her, and she could feel his breath on her shoulder, no doubt reading the directions along with her. The wind gave a gentle nudge against them, allowing Aurora to pick up the scent of seawater and mint cologne drifting past her nose.

"Ikea didn't make this, did they?" he asked, his voice tickling her ear.

Aurora stiffened a laugh. "No, I'm not big on things held together with dowels."

Gavin moved toward one of the metal rods and bent down to pick it up off the warm desert ground. As soon as his hand made contact, he dropped it like a hot potato.

"Oh, crap, that's hot enough to roast a lizard." Gavin shook his hand as though doing so would allow the heat to drip from his fingers. "It's not even noon."

"Shoot, you don't have any gloves." She hurried to him, reaching for his hand, taking it into her's. "Is your hand okay? Did it burn?"

She turned his hand over, and as he stretched out his fingers, Aurora noted the redness, but it didn't appear burned as she gently touched her fingertips to his palm.

"I don't think so, just startled me. For some reason, I didn't expect it to be so darn hot."

"Welcome to Arizona. The sun's been on those for a few hours. It doesn't take long." With his hand still in hers, Aurora gazed up against the sunshine and locked eyes with him. The current angles of their heads allowed her to narrowly make out his eyes behind the sunglasses. Her heartbeat thumped faster and louder with every passing second. The sounds of birds chirping in the creosote bushes around them seemed to go silent.

She bit her lower lip and allowed Gavin's hand to fall out of her hold.

Gavin rocked on his boots and rubbed his hands on the sides of his jeans. "I didn't pack any gloves. But maybe you have a rag or something I could use?"

"Nonsense, you can't use a rag. There are gloves back in the shed, and they should fit, they were—"

He shook his head. "No, I couldn't."

She didn't even need to say whose gloves they once were. Gavin knew, which caused more confusion in her heart.

"Honestly, he wouldn't mind, and I don't mind." Aurora hopped on the ATV so he couldn't tell her to never mind again. "I'll grab them. Do you think we need anything else?"

Gavin peered around. "Looks like you got everythin' we need."

Aurora started up the ATV and drove it back towards the shed next to the house's carport structure. The house didn't have a garage, as her grandparents mostly used horses to get around town and used the car only on rare occasions until they were older. And her parents never got around to building one, always parking their vehicles in the circle driveway. Instead, the property had an excellent shed, which was once used for farm animals during the hottest days of summer. She missed having horses, a cow, and chickens. But the care to keep up with them once Mike passed was too much for Aurora to continue with when she needed to focus on raising the girls.

Aurora braked the ATV and climbed off. Heading into the shed, she spotted the gloves at the back of the workbench. When she held them in her hand, Aurora ran her fingers over the worn sun-bleached leather. They'd been a Christmas gift from her, but the memory of which one had faded. Mike had been anything but a farm boy growing up in Phoenix. But he took to small-town life well, and soon, everyone in Woolsey forgot he was an outsider. After they married, Mike developed a great liking to all things on the property, learning what he didn't know and surprising her with something new he'd fixed or created that made life easier.

As Aurora exited the shed, her breath caught in her throat. A pair of gloves shouldn't make her cry, and she fought off the sadness pulling at the edges of her eyes. *They're only gloves.* However, as she held them in her hand, they didn't feel like gloves but a connection to what once was her happy life.

When she returned to the installation site, Gavin had wrapped the paper instructions around a rod and used it to protect his hand from the heat. As she hopped off the ATV,

Aurora noticed he'd already drilled the bolts into one of the legs.

"You're going to make me look bad if you work any faster." Aurora held out the gloves.

Gavin eased to standing and towered over her. "Thanks." He eyed the gloves. "Are you sure?"

"Of course." She waved them at him like they weren't a big deal. And she hoped he didn't see her wipe away a tear from her right eye with the back of her hand.

Aurora couldn't help staring as Gavin slid on each glove. They fit perfectly; she didn't even need to touch them to see that his hands were an exact match for her late husband's. She'd never felt more vulnerable and confused as she set her hand on the front of her neck where a lump of emotion formed in her throat.

# Chapter 8

## Gavin

"I honestly don't want to impose," Gavin said, standing in the doorway of Aurora's home. "Plus, I'm filthy."

He felt the desert's dust sandwiched between his toes, having made its way through his boots before breaching his inside-out socks. Dust coated his ears, and he could taste the grit in the back of his throat, and smelled it in his nose.

"So am I." Aurora pointed at her shirt smudged with grime.

True, she was covered with as much grit as he was, but it looked adorable on her. And he knew spending more time with her would only make matters worse—for both his heart and his mind. Not to mention he already felt bad enough about using Mike's gloves today. He knew it had affected her, watching him wear them as they put together the first windmill. Not that she said anything, but he'd spotted a tear running down her cheek, and it took a great deal of restraint not to remove the gloves and touch her tear in hopes of stopping the pain. Instead, he did what his father had taught him as a child—ignoring is the best policy when it comes to love. Ignore. Your. Feelings. Then the only person who gets hurt is you.

She grabbed at his arm and pulled it towards her. "Come in and sit down. Or better yet . . ." Aurora headed toward the kitchen, flung open the refrigerator, and hoisted up an un-opened bottle of wine. "Bust this one open."

"Bust? How does one bust open a *glass* bottle?"

She paused, holding the bottle toward Gavin. "I don't know why I said bust."

"Hopefully, it's not the first sign of heat stroke." He took the bottle from her hand.

"It's not heat stroke. I always throw random words into sentences. Sadly, much to Trinity's distaste, and if she catches me, I'm scolded for my improper use of language. The joys of having a teacher as a best friend. I'm sure the same can be said about having a judge as a longtime friend."

"More so issues with her bein' my babysitter." Gavin knew there must be more to the using odd words, perhaps nerves. When he was nervous, he'd futz around with his hat or slip his hands in and out of his pant pockets.

The glasses clanked as she set them next to each other on the island in front of him. By the time he had the cork out, the sound of the front door had swung open, followed by the scampering of feet. Coming down the hall were Willa, Ava, and Trinity.

"Hi!" Trinity called over top of the girls' heads. "They didn't have any sugar, I swear."

It was the first time he'd seen her in some time. And when she entered the kitchen, she smiled. "Gavin!"

He set the wine bottle on the counter just as Trinity wrapped her arms around him.

"Gavin knows Auntie T?" Willa climbed up onto a stool at the side of the island.

"I sure do, much to Camden's dislike," he chuckled.

Trinity gave Gavin a rub on the back, followed by a sharp pat. "I heard you were in town and wondered if you were ever going to stop by. You have to see Jolie. She's growing faster than an oleander."

"I'll be sure to stop by," Gavin mentioned.

Trinity's vision went to the wine on the counter. "Well, I'd better get outta here. If I leave Camden home alone with two dogs and Jolie long enough, it looks like a slumber party exploded by the time I get back."

"Stay, Auntie T," Willa said, spinning back and forth on the stool.

Ava grabbed her mom's hands and held them, swinging them slightly back and forth. "You're welcome to join us."

"I'd love to, but Camden and I had a rough day at school, and I'm counting on having a nice foot rub, wine, and him cooking spaghetti."

"I want spaghetti," Ava said.

"Let's say bye to Auntie T first," Aurora instructed.

Willa hopped off the barstool and hugged Trinity.

"It was great seeing you, Gavin. Please don't be a stranger; you're in Woolsey after all, so you can't hide." She leaned in and gave him another quick hug.

"Thanks, I'll stop by soon." Gavin nodded.

Aurora walked Trinity to the front door, and he couldn't make out what they were saying, although he shamefully tried to lean in that direction to hear.

"Okay, so Gavin, are you alright if I make spaghetti?" Aurora asked, coming back into the kitchen.

"Only if I can help." He poured light peach-colored Soave into each wineglass.

"Well, girls, go find something to do until dinner." Aurora reached for the glass as Gavin handed it to her. "This wine will go wonderfully with the spaghetti."

When their fingers grazed at the tips, they both paused, and their vision left their glasses and met. It was the longest second of his life, and he wanted a million more.

After they cleared the dishes from the table, Ava grabbed hold of Gavin's hand, pulling him up the stairs to her room. Aurora and Willa quickly followed behind.

"Do you have a costume for Halloween?" Ava entered her room and made a beeline for her closet doors.

"I don't." Gavin paused at the opening of the bedroom door. "Should I?"

"Yes," Willa chimed in. "Mommy has one."

"She does?" He turned to Aurora coming up the stairs.

"I do." She crossed her arms.

"I guess if I'm goin' to this haunted house thin', I have to have one then."

Ava opened her closet door and pointed at something hanging in the closet. "See, Gavin, I'm going as a unicorn!"

"I'm going to be a princess!" Willa cheered.

"Willa was a princess last year, too." Ava picked up a piece of paper from her desk and waved it in the air. "Mom, don't forget the bucket list."

"We won't. I promised," Aurora said, running her hand over the top of Willa's hair.

"What time does the haunted house start at?" Gavin inquired.

"It's a Halloween house, Gavin," Ava corrected him. "You keep saying *haunted house*."

Gavin lowered to Ava's level. "Is there a difference?"

Ava nodded her head. "Yes, the whole house is Halloween, but the haunted part is not inside the house."

"I see." Gavin placed his right fist into his left hand, cupping it.

Ava set her hand on Gavin's shoulder. "Please call it a Halloween house. That's what my daddy always called it."

"Oh." Gavin stood up and glanced back at Aurora, who appeared just as taken aback by the comment.

Aurora's face turned a shade of pale he'd not seen before. "Usually, about five thirty people start showing up." She dragged her hand down the side of her face and neck, resting it as though she was about to say the Pledge of Allegiance. "The sun sets around that time, and it makes it easier to find a parking spot without running over any jumping cholla."

"Wait, jumpin' what? Is that some kind of spider or snake?" Gavin asked.

Willa giggled. "It's a cactus!"

"Sounds like a cactus with a grudge," he responded.

Aurora pressed her lips together, muffling laughter as he smiled at her. He couldn't help but find every little thing about her more beautiful than the last thing he discovered. He only hoped that the whole haunted—*Halloween*—house wasn't going to bring back too many memories for any of the girls.

"I better get goin', let you and the girls wind down for the night." He adjusted his hat and turned to make his way to the stairs.

By the time he was at the edge of the steps, Willa had clamped onto his leg with a quick hug and then hurried back to her room. He didn't say anything as he went down the steps but hoped that he wasn't doing any damage by invading their lives.

"Do y'all carve pumpkins for Halloween?" he asked as Aurora leaned against the front door.

"We do that over at Jennifer's house." She glanced up the stairs and whispered, "The Halloween house." She shoved her right hand into the front pocket of her jeans. "The girls have been doing it there since they were little. It's really the whole town's tradition. Pumpkins go so fast in the October heat that putting them out is such a waste. And if the heat doesn't get them, the darn javelinas do. Besides, everyone in town is at Jennifer and Greg's anyways that they would never be seen by trick-or-treaters.

"Should I be concerned about these javelinas?" Gavin peered around Aurora and out the slim window next to the front door.

"No, they only like cowboys." Aurora grinned. "Oh, wait"—she pressed her pointer finger to her lip—"you're a cowboy."

Gavin felt his cheeks flush and nodded his head with a chuckle. "Okay, I see. You have jokes."

She covered her mouth with her hand, but he could still see she was smiling behind it, the way her eyes bunched up. When Aurora lowered her hand, she kept beaming, and it took a lot of strength for him not to reach out and set his hand against her cheek and press his lips to hers.

"I should go," he finally said.

Aurora looked down quickly, and then turned to open the front door. "Thank you again for your help. I couldn't have done it without you."

"You're most welcome. Thank you for supper."

"Will I see you tomorrow?" Aurora leaned on the door-frame, her hand resting on the knob.

"Absolutely. Have a good night." Gavin willed his feet to move—to descend the few porch steps onto the gravel.

"You too," she said but didn't close the front door.

"I can't leave until you shut and lock the door." He glanced at the disappearing sunset in the distance and then back around to Aurora. "That way, I know you're safe."

"You don't have to worry about me. I'm a big girl."

That's exactly what worried him. "I wouldn't be a Southern gentleman if I left and found out something happened. I heard about the javelinas."

She stepped outside, leaving the door open. "Well then, I should be the one making sure you make it to your truck safely."

He chuckled. "Good night, Aurora."

"Good night, cowboy." And with that, the door shut.

# Chapter 9

## Aurora

Aurora sat on the last step of the staircase as the sound of Gavin's truck disappeared down the road outside. She folded her head into her hands and took several deep breaths. While desperately needing Gavin's help to get the windmills up and running, she didn't need anything else from him. She wanted it, though—and there was a difference.

The most important thing in Aurora's life was to make sure her girls understood that their mom could take care of them and that another man wouldn't just come and go. And that was precisely what Gavin would be doing, even if not intentional. She remained on the step and reminded herself that all she had to do was focus on keeping the relationship with Gavin strictly business. After all, that's all it could be. And in order to do that, she'd need to pay him for his assistance. Sure, he had said he didn't want payment, but it would take any relationship expectations entirely out of the picture. Yet, the fall bucket list confused things a bit.

Aurora stood and headed to the kitchen to retrieve her cell phone. After pouring herself a smidge of Soave, eyeballing the glass, and adding a smidge more, she called Trinity.

"How much should I pay Gavin?" Aurora asked, not bothering with a hello. The line was silent. Aurora pulled her phone away from her ear to make sure the call hadn't dropped. "Trin?"

"Yeah, I'm here," Trinity said. "But what exactly are you paying Gavin . . . for?"

"For helping me set up the windmills." Aurora pressed her elbows onto the island.

"Oh, okay. Well, in that case—"

"What did you think I was referring to for payment?" Aurora's hand went up like it was holding a serving tray. "Wait, I don't want to know." She rolled her eyes and sipped her wine.

Trinity laughed. "Sorry, I'm not sure why my mind went there. Too many reality love shows."

"Maybe I should call R. J. instead."

"R. J. is not equipped to safely do anything. One wrong move, and he'll probably pull his back again."

"I guess you're about R. J. Anyways, I would say maybe a hundred bucks a day, give or take. Construction workers make around twenty an hour. At least that's what the Hackenbergs paid for their new addition."

"I can swing that," Aurora mentioned.

The sound of gravel under tires was audible in the distance, and she hurried to the side window by the front door to see who was driving around. "Hey, speaking of R. J., what's he doing?"

"R. J.?"

"Yeah, his truck, it just passed by, and since I doubt he's lost, that means he's going to your mom's house."

"Very interesting. I guess we have ourselves a continued love triangle between my mom, R. J., and the judge. And with Gavin in town, maybe we can finally get to the bottom of it."

"This triangle has been going on since Elizabeth arrived, has it not?" Aurora returned to the living room couch and sat down.

"You'd think at their age they'd stop dragging it out. Anyways, onto more important matters. I thought Gavin was helping out, and it wasn't a business transaction, only luck that brought him here at the right time?"

"I don't think he finds a Category 4 hurricane lucky."

"You know what I mean. And I saw the way he looked at you when I dropped off the girls. Catching glances at you like he was in junior high school." Trinity laughed.

"Oh gosh." Aurora felt her cheeks warm.

"Mom!" Ava's voice echoed through the house. "Mom!"

Aurora took a quick sip of Soave and set the glass on the coffee table. "Gotta go, have a great night, bye."

"Bye."

Aurora tapped the end icon on the cell, and it felt like a *Saved by the Bell* moment as she hurried toward the stairs. Jogging up the steps, Aurora entered Ava's room to find it empty. "Ava?"

"Mom in here, look what Willa did." Ava pointed at her sister.

Willa had managed to get her tiny desk chair from her room into Aurora's bathroom and had used it to get the makeup out of the top vanity drawer. Her youngest daughter stood on the chair and looked at her mom using the mirror over her shoulder.

"She put on your makeup. We're not supposed to be playing in the bathroom." Ava crossed her arms. "Mom, she's in trouble, right?"

Aurora covered her mouth to prevent her girls from seeing her laugh. Burgundy lipstick smeared over Willa's lips in a clown-like circle, and she'd rubbed smoky gray shadow across her lids nearly to her ears and up to the tops of her eyebrows.

"Mommy, look!" Willa cheered and produced a Joker-style grin.

"Honey, you know you're not supposed to be playing with my makeup."

"I'm not playing. I'm pretty." Willa leaned closer to the mirror. "Mommy, we have to look pretty for Gavin."

Aurora's heart pinched in her chest. "Why do we have to be pretty for Gavin?" She scooped up Willa and held her in a hug on her hip.

"Because we like him." Willa touched her lips and pulled her stained fingers back to examine them.

And that was precisely what Aurora was afraid of, for all of them.

# Chapter 10

## Gavin

Even after spending the entire day with Aurora, Gavin's heartbeat sped up as he drove over to her house after stopping to clean up and change into his costume. They'd finished constructing the first windmill and hadn't run into any issues. His biggest problem was making sure she didn't catch him staring at her, which proved more difficult than he'd imagined. It was as though he'd been stranded on an island alone for a year, and Aurora was the first sign of life he'd seen.

Gavin enjoyed spending time with her, but it was more than time that caused his heart to race—although when it did it was freeing, like riding a motorcycle. She made him focus on what was right in front of him without even saying a word.

The gravel crunched under the truck's tires as he pulled into the drive of Aurora's house. On the horizon, he spotted the windmill; its vane and wind wheel moving with the breeze. He took in the land as he stepped from the truck and made his way to the front door. It was an impressive piece of acreage with the small airplane hangar turned carport at the edge of the house. Upon closer inspection, the carport had worn in places, as was the house's siding. A layer of tan filtered over everything, muting its worn self to those who looked too quickly.

Aurora's front door opened, and a bouncing unicorn stumbled out.

"Gavin, what are you supposed to be?" Ava asked. "You look the same."

Next, a princess in a purple tutu and puffy sleeves walked out the front door.

"He's a cowboy!" Willa laughed.

"He's *always* a cowboy," Ava stated with disapproval.

Before he could plead his case to the girls, colors of gold, red, and blue drew his vision up above the girls' heads. Aurora stood there in a Wonder Woman costume that showcased just how hard she worked keeping up with her daughters and the two hundred acres.

"What? Does this look bad?" Aurora ran her hand over the front of her costume.

Gavin's mouth went drier than the desert around him. He swallowed. "No, you look wonderful."

A smile spread across Aurora's face. "Thank you." She locked the door, and her shiny red boots made their way toward him. "I wasn't sure, I mean, it's a lot of skin to be showing off, but I figured it's going to be dark." Gavin nodded, still mesmerized by her. "Thanks for coming over. I figured it would be better if we all took one car. That way, if you want to drink or something, I can drop you off at the judge's house." Aurora headed towards the vehicle.

Gavin followed them around to the side of the 4Runner and caught Aurora's slender arm muscles on display as she hoisted Willa up into her booster seat while the unicorn climbed in. "Oh, shoot the pumpkins."

Aurora jogged back to the house, and he had to stare. He couldn't stop himself. Wonder Woman was running away from him. He hurried after her to help carry two giant pumpkins while she relocked the front door and cradled two smaller pumpkins.

"You didn't have to get me one," he said, loading them into the back of the 4Runner.

"Yes, I did. Plus, the girls insisted. They said you would be a poop-poop head if you didn't carve one with us."

"Well, I'd hate to have poop-poop head added to my ré-sumé." Gavin held open the driver's side door as Aurora slid inside.

"Why, aren't you a gentleman."

He tipped his hat, winked, and made his way to the passenger door.

"You know, technically, you're a cowboy every day, so that doesn't count as a costume." Aurora turned the key.

"I could say the same thing about you." The line was corny, and he knew it, but being cheesy in front of her didn't matter. He couldn't help himself. *Bring on the macaroni, there's plenty more cheesiness where that came from.* When he glanced over at her, he noticed a slight grin remained on her lips.

About five minutes later, when Aurora pulled off the side of the road, Gavin could tell this was the place to be for Halloween. Multiple glowing jack-o'-lanterns lined both sides of the driveway leading to the single-story ranch-style home. Every window displayed wooden boards crossing haphazardly over them with yellow caution tape and tombstones of all sizes spread across the ground under a nearby tree. Giant black spiders hung from the tree branches and the porch's roofline.

Aurora clutched a gigantic bag of mixed chocolate candy and grabbed the smaller pumpkins from the back, while Gavin carried the two bigger ones.

The wide-open garage sat to the left of the home, and "The Monster Mash" drifted out of it as the purple-and-orange lights blinked across the front. Large-scale skeletons hung from either side of the garage's entrance.

Ava's hand wrapped itself around Gavin's as they walked closer to the crowd milling in the middle of the driveway. "Gavin, come with me into the haunted house," she said, tugging at his hand.

"If it's alright with your mom." He glanced over at Wonder Woman and Willa.

"Of course, go have fun. I hate going into that thing anyway." Aurora added her bag of candy to the large bucket.

"What about Willa?" Gavin asked.

"No, thank you!" Willa stated and grabbed her mom's hand.

"Neither of us are into scary stuff." Aurora glanced down at Willa and gave her a thumb-up. "Have fun!"

Ava continued to pull Gavin across the driveway as his vision turned to a structure that looked unsafe but was clearly part of the plan. It had a tunnel-like opening high enough for kids to go through, but adults would need to hunch over.

"Are you sure about this, Ava?" Gavin braced his boots into the dirt below, causing them to freeze at the entrance.

"Gavin, you're a cowboy. Cowboys can't be scared." Ava pulled at his hand again.

"Okay, but don't let go of my hand."

The tunnel grew dark instantly as they entered what appeared to be PVC pipes draped in black fabric. It was a grand structure that could quickly be taken down and stored until it was needed again. The path snaked with sharp corners as Ava held tight to Gavin's hand. Her tiny fingers wrapped around his index and pinky finger, tugging at parts of his heart he'd forgot existed.

They continued through the pitch-black passageway until they were hit in the face with what must have been silly string. Ava screamed and squeezed tighter to Gavin's hand. When they went around the next curve, a skeleton swung forward in front of them, stopping them in their tracks. He screamed along with Ava, which caused her to laugh.

"It scared you too, Gavin!" She readjusted her fingers around his hand as they moved past the skeleton and farther forward.

A greenish glow appeared on the ground in front of them. At first glance, it looked one hundred percent real, but stepping closer, he noticed it was a well-planned square hole in the ground with a grate cover over plastic snakes and a green light. Ava held tight as they crossed it together.

Around the next corner were all sizes of hanging eyeballs, and they ducked and weaved to get through. As soon as they turned another corner of the tunnel, they ran smack dab into a group of dangling spiders. Ava screamed and ran forward, taking Gavin's two fingers with her, nearly yanking them out of the sockets.

"That was so fun!" she said as they stood at the edge of the tunnel, back out in the open air of the night.

"It was. Thanks for helping me get through it. You were brave," Gavin said, looking down at this hand and seeing Ava was still holding it.

"Let's go find my mom. I want to carve the pumpkin."

Gavin spotted Aurora in a sea of townspeople, surrounded by a ghost, a witch, a pirate, and an adult princess. Kids ran around, burning off their sugar high, making it hard to determine what some of their costumes were. Yet with Aurora, it was like a spotlight was on her, and everything else blurred. She had a black cup in one hand and her other was tucked tight to her body.

"Hey, cowboy," Aurora said as they approached.

He was grateful it was dark out because he was pretty sure he'd never before blushed the way he was right then in his entire life.

"Mom, let's carve pumpkins," Ava said, still holding his hand. "Gavin, you have to, too. We got you a pumpkin."

"Go get your sister, please." Aurora pointed at a group of little ones sitting in front of a makeshift white sheet screen watching Halloween-themed cartoons.

The garage had long tables set up running in the shape of a U. All kinds of carving tools littered the area, making it look like a surgery party was about to happen.

"Where are the templates?" he asked Aurora, who wedged the girls between them.

"Templates?" she snickered. "I'm not sure what happens in your neck of the woods, but here in Woolsey, it's all freehand."

"Y'all are goin' to regret that bein' an option when I'm done." Gavin lifted his pumpkin in both hands.

Aurora turned to him, and he had to remind his jaw to keep from dropping to the floor of the garage. The Wonder Woman costume didn't help dampen his infatuation. If they were back in the Midwest someplace or even the Pacific Northwest, she'd have to throw a coat on to stay warm. But here, it must've been at least eighty degrees out.

As much as he hated to, he returned to focusing on his pumpkin and what he might possibly carve. His eyes wandered the garage to see if he could gather any ideas.

Aurora popped off the top of her pumpkin. "My most favorite part!" She shoved her hand inside the belly of the pumpkin and withdrew a wad of guts.

"You're the first woman I've ever met who likes that. I don't even like *that*." He winced at the thought, his hand nowhere near the inside of the pumpkin.

Aurora used her right hand to scoop out more seeds while her other held the pumpkin firmly on the table. As Gavin yanked the cut top off his pumpkin, he caught something out of the corner of his eye. Coming at him was Aurora, with a handful of pumpkin guts.

"They're so slimy," she oozed, hoisting them closer to Gavin's face.

He raised his hands in defense. "Stay away from me!" His tone was loud, yet joking. Gavin stepped backward as Aurora inched closer.

"You're not scared, are you?" Aurora grinned.

Smiles formed on Willa and Ava's faces.

"Mom's going to get you, Gavin," Willa warned.

"You're an evil woman, you know that?" Gavin shook his finger at her.

"No, Gavin, she's Wonder Woman," Willa stated.

All it took was a tiny lunge from Aurora, and the pumpkin goop was far too close for Gavin's comfort. He jumped backward. However, it was too late. She shoved the pumpkin mess into both his hands. He gritted his teeth. "I'm okay. I don't mind." Every muscle in his body tightened.

The pumpkin goop fell near his boots, and Aurora grabbed his dirty hand. "I promise you won't die. Now come on, I'll help you scoop out your pumpkin, you big baby."

With Aurora standing next to him, their arms touching, he could smell the scent of vanilla and nutmeg. Was it possible for a person to smell like fall? And for the first time in his life, autumn became his favorite season.

# Chapter 11

## Aurora

After wiping off her makeup with a hot washcloth, Aurora tucked her girls in for the night and snuck two chocolates from Willa's treat bag. Then, running her hand down the handrail, she made her way into the kitchen and poured herself some pinot noir before snuggling into the couch's plush cushions.

Turning on the TV, she thought about how to approach the subject of paying Gavin. This morning when they worked together was a perfect time, but she'd been too distracted between her attraction to him and trying to get the second windmill built. And she hadn't felt it was appropriate to bring it up at the Halloween party. To be honest, it made her nervous to approach the subject, again. He'd already told her he should pay her for giving him something to do while he's in Woolsey. Aurora didn't want to offend him, and either way, it felt as though she might.

Thankfully she'd already loaded *Ghostbusters*, as per her yearly Halloween tradition, into the DVD player because she'd found the perfect position between the couch pillows and didn't want to move. But before the Columbia Pictures opening even faded from the screen, her cell phone rang.

Aurora reached for it on the couch's armrest. "Hi, Gavin."

"Hi, sorry, I hope I'm not buggin' you."

"Not at all. I was just starting a movie." Aurora hit pause on the remote.

"I wanted to thank you for such a pleasant time tonight."

"The girls and I had so much fun."

"It was enjoyable to do something new." The line was silent. "What movie did I interrupt?"

"*Ghostbusters.*"

"What a classic. Wait, it's the original one, right?

"Of course."

"I haven't seen that one in ages." Gavin's voice went up in a cheerful tone.

"Want to come over and watch it with me?"

"Are you sure? I don't want to wake the girls."

"My girls can sleep through a tornado."

The sound of gravel in the drive alerted Aurora to Gavin's arrival, and she sprang from the couch and hurried to the door. A flurry of both excitement and panic warred in her stomach as she stepped back and allowed him to enter.

"I figured I should bring this." Gavin held up a bottle of sauvignon blanc. "And this," he whispered.

"Perfect." Her eyes rested on the bag of candy. "Hey, where's your hat?"

"I didn't want to overdo my cowboyness."

She looked back over her shoulder and laughed as he followed her into the kitchen. Pulling a wineglass down for him, she poured him a glass of pinot noir and set the bottle he'd brought in the refrigerator.

"We'll open this next. Mine's still full." Aurora pointed at her glass on the coffee table.

Gavin traded the wineglass she handed him for the bag of assorted chocolate bars full of caramel and nugget. The movie remained paused on the television as they sank into the couch, keeping about a foot of space between them.

"I paused it as soon as I knew you were coming over so we could watch it together from the beginning." Aurora held the remote in her hand.

"Thank you." Gavin took a sip of wine, and the light off the television reflected in his eyes as Aurora gazed into them over her glass. It was a full moon tonight, and the glow streaming in through the French doors helped illuminate the living room.

"So, you don't allow your girls to watch this?" Gavin turned to her.

"No. I'm *that* parent. I'm worried they'll have nightmares. Maybe next Halloween I'll let Ava join me."

She didn't know if it was the warmth of the wine or having Gavin's company, but she felt utterly cozy at the moment, even without all the pillows. It was the first time since Mike's passing that she'd shared a movie with or sat on the couch next to a man. The realization of this caused Aurora's breathing to deepen. Her desire to be comforted by him with a touch, a closeness, fogged-up her thoughts. Was it so wrong to want the sides of their legs to touch or wish to lean her head on his shoulder?

Except for the crinkle of candy wrappers opening, they remained silent as the movie played. And when Aurora's heartbeat flooded her ears with loud thumps, she was grateful Gavin couldn't hear. Finally, she turned to him when the credits rolled, noticing his wineglass was as empty as hers.

"Shoot, we never opened your wine." Aurora wiggled her empty glass in front of her. "I usually watch *Sleepy Hollow* next, but if you need to get going, please don't feel obligated to stay."

"I don't think I've seen that one before."

Aurora stood up, straightening out her legs, stiff from sitting for almost two hours. "It's a great one, just scary enough." She reached her hands up in a stretch toward the ceiling.

"I'd like to stay if that's okay. I don't want to overstep, but I know Lizzy is probably still at Jennifer's house, and I could use the company. Don't get me wrong, Lizzy is great, but she'll always feel like my babysitter in some form or another, and I want to keep eatin' candy and stay up past my bedtime." He smiled like a child who'd gotten away with sneaking something from a secret stash candy drawer.

"You have a bedtime?" Aurora grabbed Gavin's wineglass off the coffee table.

His eyes narrowed in thought. "When you work in construction, gettin' in the habit of wakin' with the sun and goin' to bed with it tends to happen."

"I guess I sort of have a scheduled bedtime too, because of the girls." She set the empty wineglasses on the island. "Can I ask you something?"

"Shoot." Gavin turned, looking over the back of the couch towards the kitchen.

"Have you ever lost anyone?" She didn't mean to be so forward, but between the wine and the late night, her curiosity had gotten the best of her.

She popped the cork on the sauvignon blanc and filled their glasses half full. Gavin remained on the couch, but his head had turned to the French doors.

"I'm sorry, that's none of my business." Aurora's bare feet smacked the tile floor as she approached the couch and handed him the glass.

Gavin took it and shook his head. "Nothin' wrong with the question. Everyone grieves in different ways when they lose someone."

She removed *Ghostbusters* from the player and slid in *Sleepy Hollow*. "That's not answering my question."

He stared off toward the bookcases flanking the television and then scratched at the crown of his head. Aurora returned to her spot on the couch, bringing both legs to her chest, and set the wineglass on her right knee, holding it at the stem.

She turned and reached for his arm, her fingers grazing it before sitting back. "Forget I asked."

As she hit play on *Sleepy Hollow*, Aurora's face drained of color, and she could feel it under her skin. How could she ask him a personal question like that? Being around Gavin made it seem as though they were childhood friends who could discuss anything and everything.

Gavin leaned toward her and took the remote from her hand, hitting pause. "I've lost people I loved, but never a spouse. Do you want to talk about it?"

She did. She wanted to talk to someone who didn't live in town, that didn't look at her like a lost puppy. She loved everything about Woolsey, but it sometimes suffocated her and her emotions. If she so much as cried, someone found out about it and bombarded her with apologetic looks.

"I miss Mike immensely, and when I think about it, it catches in my breath, and I nearly choke. Yet, at the same time, I miss being loved and in love. I desire a new start for my girls and myself. And I crave to be rescued from my emotions and thoughts."

"The guilt you're battlin' is a lot."

She sipped the wine, and it took all her effort to swallow it over the lump that'd developed in her throat. "I want so much for my girls, and I know I can give them what they need, but I also know they're missing their father and missing so much from that relationship. We want things to be normal again when we know they never will."

"What about makin' you and the girls' lives what *you* want by forgettin' what you assume you should be doin'?" Gavin set his glass on the coffee table and rested his elbows on his knees. "I understand in a small town it's hard to look past what you think you should do and simply do what you need. Jesser Parish isn't much bigger than Woolsey. And I can't tell you how Mike would want you to feel or what he would expect, but I'm sure this town has already forced their opinions on you enough."

Aurora nodded and wiped a single tear rolling down her cheek. "They have."

"I promise you'll know when the time is right for you. The only one who can decide that is you. Even the girls, they'll let you know if they're not ready or if they are. Love doesn't have a date or time, it's a feelin', and you'll know it when it breaks away the hurt from your heart. Slowly, that pit in the back of your throat, connecting to your stomach, will soften and disappear."

He was right, and she knew it as she reached out for his arm and squeezed it, letting her fingers linger before sitting back on the couch.

"You know Willa and Ava enjoyed having you with us tonight. Ava wouldn't stop talking about the haunted tunnel. She's looking forward to our fall bucket list, mostly because you'll be partaking. I hope you're still up for it."

"Absolutely. I can't wait."

"She took the list with her to bed. It's on her nightstand. I was going to have her cross off pumpkin carving and the haunted house, but she wanted to wait until you two could do

65

it together. I know it sounds silly, but it means a lot to her. For some reason, the list is like a lifeline to normal."

"Why do you say that?"

"Because when we got home, she couldn't find the list and became frantic searching for it."

"Was it like that last year?"

"Last year was our first fall without Mike, and we missed out on a few traditions. We went through the motions, but some things were simply too hard."

"Did you still watch your movies?"

"Let's just say I woke up on the couch with the movies still in the box, a stomachache, and candy wrappers stuck to my face."

Gavin held up his right hand. "I promise this year I'll make sure you don't have any wrappers stuck on you."

Aurora giggled and hiccupped. "Excuse me." She hiccupped again.

He laughed. "Does this happen a lot?"

"No." She hiccupped. "Oh, for goodness' sake."

"I don't think *Sleepy Hollow* will be scary with you hiccupping."

She waved him off and hit play on the movie. "Don't be silly. They'll go"—she hiccupped—"away soon."

Shadows moved outside of the French doors and back windows in the yard. Aurora jumped, almost spilling her wine.

"What was that?" Gavin simultaneously set his wineglass on the table and stood. He moved toward the French doors, his stance strong and assured. Aurora eased off the couch and made her way toward him, standing close enough behind she could smell his minty-wood scent. Of course, nothing dangerous ever happened in Woolsey, even on Halloween, but Aurora doubted this between the wine and the sugar rush.

"You stay here. I'll go check it out." Gavin reached for the doorknob and unlocked it.

"Wait," she whispered, and set her hand on top of his.

When her palm made contact with his skin, tingles traveled up her arm like lightning bolts.

"What?" He turned to her, their faces mere inches apart.

His vision drew away from her eyes and moved to her lips. She swallowed. "It's okay." Aurora pointed outside. In the distance, beyond the desert willows, a wild horse stood, followed by two more. "They're at the water bucket I set out. It's an important reminder of how vital those windmills will be."

"I guess I don't get to play the cowboy in shiny armor tonight." His hand slid from the doorknob.

She pouted. "Such a shame."

And it *really* was.

# Chapter 12

## Gavin

Gavin removed his boots and carried them through the living room at Lizzy's house well into the morning of November 1. He'd finished watching *Sleepy Hollow* with Aurora around one, and the entire town was dark on his drive back, as was the judge's house when he tiptoed to the guest room.

Just as he made it to the room, Lizzy's bedroom door popped open. She remained mostly behind it, the soft light escaping onto the floor below. "Fun night?"

Gavin pivoted around. "Yes, I'm sorry if I woke you."

"Pish-posh, I only got home fifteen minutes ago."

"Oh, what kept you out so late?" Gavin leaned against the guest bedroom door.

"R. J. and I got to chattin'. The spiced cider might've gone to my head a little." She held up her hand, showing off her pincer grasp. "Lillian was flirtin' with him somethin' fierce when I showed up at the Halloween party."

"Flirtin'?" Gavin set his boots on the floor next to the entrance of the bedroom door.

"Maybe. I'm not sure. They always seem cozy together. Of course, they're longtime friends, but at times it seems like more."

"Do I sense a love triangle?" He clicked on the light switch.

68

"Please, this is not *General Hospital*. If R. J. liked me, we would've gone on more than two dates in six months' time. I don't understand why he doesn't either make it official with Lillian or at least stop givin' me hope."

"You've been on dates?" Gavin crossed his arms.

"Don't you start with me. It's late. And I'm goin' to bed. Good night." Lizzy shut her door.

"Night," Gavin said, closing his door, even though she probably couldn't hear him.

After he readied himself for sleep, he sat on the edge of the bed, the mattress bowing. He hadn't been completely honest with Aurora tonight. But there was nothing he could do about it, and he didn't want it to be about him because it didn't matter. *Can't change the past.*

He, too, had lost someone close—two people, in fact. Mila had captured his heart, as had her four-year-old son, Jax. The accident happened during last year's hurricane—Lorenzo, not nearly as bad as this year's, but a hurricane all the same. Mila refused to leave her home. She'd worked hard for it and didn't take the weather seriously. He'd warned her, and then, when it was too late to leave, he'd tried to save her and Jax.

As he closed his eyes, he could still see the little boy and his mom. No matter how much time had passed, whenever he closed his eyes, he saw their faces. And *even if* he was falling for Aurora and *even if* she was ready, he couldn't be in a relationship with someone who had children.

Gavin slid open the bedroom window, allowing the cool air to pass through the screen. Sounds of crickets trickled in as he rested his arms on the sill, his nose close enough to the screen to catch the slight scent of dust trapped in it. There wasn't much to look at in the darkness outside of the shadow given off by the moon against a cactus.

Lowering himself onto the bed, he removed his cell phone. Going to the photo icon, he scrolled through to the two photos he'd taken earlier in the evening—both of Aurora and her girls; one with them holding their carved pumpkins and one with all four of them. Then, without thinking, he scrolled too far in the opposite direction, bringing up the oldest photos on his phone—a photo of Mila and Jax during a camping trip. Jax had caught a catfish nearly the size of his head, and Gavin let out a short chuckle seeing it again. He'd lost count of how many times he almost deleted the photos, his thumb hovering over the small trash can icon. But something always stopped him. He didn't want to erase the memories; he only wanted to erase the hurt.

Exiting out of the photo gallery, he rested his phone on his chest and closed his eyes. As sleep fell over him, he forced his mind to eradicate the pictures of the past and fill them with the memories created today. Although Aurora and he could never be, their relationship between the windmill and the water tanks needed to remain. At least for now, he could work on finally moving away from the daily memories of Mila and Jax.

# Chapter 13

## Aurora

"Isn't it bad luck to make a pumpkin pie outside of Thanksgiving?" Gavin stood in front of Aurora's kitchen island.

"Where did you hear that?" Aurora asked, stirring the condensed milk into the mixing bowl.

"The . . . the *Fall Guide to Good Luck*." Gavin raised his right eyebrow.

"Gavinnnn," Willa declared, leaning forward on the island as she wiggled back and forth on the barstool. "Mom, is that true?"

"Of course not. It's November. We can make pumpkin pie without any worries. Now, what's on the bucket list for us to do next?"

"De ... dco ... Mom." Ava pointed with her finger. "I forgot how to say it."

Aurora leaned over and looked at the list upside down. "Decorate."

"Decorate! Your po-por-porch! Can we do that?"

"Yes, that's a great idea." Aurora smiled, thinking about how she should have had Ava do more of the writing to learn the words on her bucket list.

"It's after Halloween. What's there to decorate?" Gavin allowed Willa to spin the pair of them around in circles as she held his hands. "Besides, if you leave pumpkins out, wild animals will eat them."

"Wild cows will eat them!" Willa said.

"Wild cows?" Gavin asked.

"Willa calls the cows that wander away from the farms wild. Sometimes they wander through our yard and rub their flanks against the gazebo. Or once I left my 4Runner out, and they took out a side mirror. And yes, the javelinas will eat them for sure. But not the plastic ones. Or paper ones. We can make them and stick them in the windows."

"Mom, it says to decorate the porch, not the windows."

"Sorry, okay." Aurora held up both of her hands. "But I don't think that Charlie will have any fake pumpkins at his store."

"Can we go to the city? Please? And get ice cream cones!"

"How about we make ice cream?" Gavin faced the girls.

"You can *make* ice cream?" Willa shrieked. "Mom, can you *make* ice cream?"

Aurora looked at Gavin, and he mouthed *sorry*. "Yes, you can," she answered her daughter.

"How can you call yourself country if you don't know how to make ice cream?" Gavin asked.

"Because we don't have an ice cream maker." Aurora poured the pumpkin pie mix into the crust-covered glass pie pan.

"Lizzy does. And I know she'll let y'all borrow it." Gavin approached the oven.

"Can we make pumpkin ice cream?" Ava asked, with a grin as wide as a jack-o'-lantern.

Aurora slowly lifted the pie pan off the counter and stepped toward the oven as Gavin opened the door. "Don't you think that's too much pumpkin, sweetie?"

"No," both Ava and Gavin chimed in at the same time.

Aurora laughed as she slid the pie into the preheated oven. "Okay, pumpkin ice cream it is then."

Gavin closed the door for Aurora and then went over to high-five Ava before kneeling to high-fived Willa. "Yay!" he said.

There was so much joy in the room that Aurora could almost see it in the air. When Gavin was with them, things didn't feel broken. Sure, they weren't complete, exactly. But they were someplace in the middle, and she accepted that was enough for now. Someplace better than before, and it was a good place to be.

"Girls, why don't you go watch some cartoons." Aurora wrang a dish towel in her hands.

Gavin stood on the other side of the kitchen island as the girls turned their attention to the living room television.

"I wanted to talk to you about payment," Aurora nearly whispered.

He slid onto a barstool. "Payment for?"

She tucked her hair behind both ears. "For your help with the windmills."

"I thought we discussed this?" Gavin crossed his arms.

Aurora spun around and busied herself with soaking the mixing bowl and measuring cups. "We did," she said over her shoulder, "but I don't want to complicate . . . I don't want . . ."

Gavin stood and walked over to the sink. With each step closer, her heartbeat raced. She desperately wanted to take the faucet hose and douse herself with cold water.

When he set his hand next to hers on the sink's lip, their skin touched, and shivers vibrated through her arm. She was suddenly grateful for wearing long sleeves so Gavin couldn't see the goose bumps that popped up.

"I don't mean to complicate anything," Gavin softly said.

She turned to him, looking up. "Oh, I'm not blaming you. I just—"

"I'm sorry if being here is causin' any complications. We'll keep it about the business."

Her eyes squinted at what Gavin had said, and she looked down at the sink. *That was easier than expected.*

"Mom!" Willa shouted from the couch. "We have to do the next thing on the list with Gavin. The leaves!"

Aurora pressed her lips together and glanced around Gavin. Then, feeling the heat dissipate, she reached behind him and snatched the list off the counter.

"How exactly will we be able to see fall leaves?" Gavin pointed at the paper.

"Up north," Aurora mentioned.

"We're driving to Montana?"

Aurora smacked his arm, unable to control her reflex. "No, Flagstaff or Prescott."

"We don't have to leave the state?"

"You have a lot to learn about Arizona, cowboy."

Watching Gavin's lips turn up into a smile, she pressed her hand into the edge of the counter at the sink. She wanted to explore the unknown with Gavin, but something changed since last night. They'd been headed in such a great direction, but now . . . Had bringing up the money for work with the windmills caused a divide? Or was reality setting in for them both?

# Chapter 14

## Gavin

Gavin angled Aurora's 4Runner into the parking spot at the bottom of the trailhead. The drive took about three hours to the location the girls had picked out, with the help of their mom. He knew it was a bad idea to continue hanging out with them, but he couldn't bring himself to keep it only about the business no matter how many internal pep talks he had with himself.

"I can already see the beautiful fall colors." Aurora leaned toward the dashboard.

Outside the vehicle was an abundance of gold, yellow, and lime-green leaves.

"Well, look at that. Fall." Gavin popped open the driver's side door.

"It's beautiful." Aurora helped Willa out of her booster seat, and Ava jumped down by herself.

"Okay, girls, no wandering off. We're hunting for fall leaves that are on the ground. Don't pull any off the trees. Then, when we get home, we can do a fun art project with them." Aurora straightened Willa's jacket.

The air was crisp, sending an unexpected shiver through Gavin's body. Of course he'd only packed T-shirts and light button-down shirts. It was Arizona, after all. He rubbed at his arms with his hands.

"Here." Aurora's arm stretched out toward him, holding a navy-blue sweater in her grip.

"Thanks, I might be slightly chilly." As he took it from her, he couldn't help but notice it was clearly a man's sweater. It must've been Mike's, and he vowed not to put it on unless his teeth chattered. Tucking it under his arm, he followed Aurora and the girls to the start of the trailhead marked by a wooden sign.

Willa stopped and grabbed Gavin's hand. "That's my dad's sweater."

"I promise to take good care of it." He struggled to swallow down the unexpected pain rising in his throat.

"He would want you to wear it if you get cold." Willa looked up at him. "Are you going to collect leaves, too?"

"Of course." Gavin smiled. "But you'll have to help me. Since I'm tall and the leaves are low, I'll probably miss all the good ones."

Willa laughed. "You *are* tall. Taller than my dad."

Gavin pressed his lips together, only to let out a long, deep breath. There was nothing to respond with; it sucked for Aurora and her girls, and even if he said something, what could he possibly say? Nothing anyone said in Jesser ever helped him miss Mila and Jax any less. Sometimes it made it worse, bringing those feelings up to the surface.

The trailhead snaked a corner, and a bridge made of painted brown steel led the path deeper into the colors associated with autumn.

"Aurora, how about I take your picture with the girls?" He pointed at the bridge.

"We'd love that, thank you. It's been a long time since we took a photo as a—" Her vision drifted to the girls and then to her boots.

He suddenly hated that he'd mentioned taking a photo in the first place.

Aurora stood at the start of the bridge, setting her hands on Ava and Willa's shoulders. But seeing her with her girls brought a smile upon his lips because Mike's life lived on in them.

He held his cell phone, portrait style. "One, two, pumpkin ice cream," he said.

The girls all laughed, and he captured it in the shot.

"Mom, what about Gavin?" Willa asked.

Before Aurora could answer, Gavin interjected, "No, it's okay."

"You don't want to be in our photo?" Willa frowned.

Gavin's heart split in two. "No, Willa. It's . . ." *Think quick!*

"Honey," Aurora lowered herself to Willa's eye level and took her hand. "It's not that, it's—"

"We don't have anyone to take our photo," Gavin sputtered.

"You can put it on that rock," Ava pointed.

"Ava has a point." Aurora stood up and faced him.

He looked where Ava directed and spotted a boulder about waist high behind him. Gavin propped the phone up against it and walked backward toward the girls.

He wedged his way between Willa and Ava and was suddenly aware of his hands, as though he had never used them in his life and didn't know what they were for. Should he shove them in his pockets, or place an arm around Aurora? Before he could make heads or tails of the situation, Aurora moved closer to him, their arms touching. He looked toward his phone and smiled.

"Photo!" he yelled.

Aurora shook as she laughed. "Photo?"

"It's what I had programmed in for the voice command to take the picture."

"What happened to *smile* or *cheese*?" Aurora tilted her head toward him, the light filtering around her hair.

"Do you know how many times I say cheese in a day?" Gavin turned to her.

"Apparently, a lot."

"Therefore, if I'm sayin' cheese, then who knows how many unauthorized pictures I'd be takin'."

"Your camera app has to be open for it to work." Aurora smiled but kept her vision toward the phone.

"Either way, risky move." Gavin shifted in his boots.

"Okay, then what's wrong with *smile*?"

The grin remained on his face. "Maybe I want a serious photo and don't want to smile, therefore saying smile would defeat the meaning of the photo."

"Who likes a serious photo?" Aurora crossed her arms.

Gavin turned to her, forgetting about the picture. "Well, for starters, there's a large population of cranky cats who refuse to smile for photos."

"You take a lot of photos with hostile cats?" Aurora's brow creased.

"Yes, don't you?" Gavin couldn't keep a straight face, and the laughter spilled out.

"Photo!" Aurora yelled but didn't turn to look at the cell phone.

He was lost in her eyes; they pulled him in like a sinkhole that he never wanted to fight his way out from.

"Come on, no-smile-no-cheese man, let's go." Aurora pivoted on her heels in the opposite direction.

Gavin retrieved his phone and caught up to the girls crossing the bridge. "I'm taken aback by the difference a few hours' drive makes. I honestly never thought I'd see anythin' fall here."

"I'm glad we're proving you wrong, then." Aurora glanced over at him and smiled as they continued on the dirt trail.

He wanted her to prove him wrong about everything in life. But mostly, he wanted Aurora to prove that he could find a way to move past the memory of what happened to Jax and Mila, and reassure himself, somehow, that the girls would never endure the same fate. Aurora had already unknowingly confirmed that he could fall in love again because no matter how much he fought it, it was happening.

# Chapter 15

## Aurora

Aurora handed Trinity a nearly overflowing glass of malbec, and they made their way to the couch. The girls were over at Lillian's house having a sleep over with Jolie.

"Having my mom next door to you really is the best thing." Trinity sipped some wine without even needing to tilt the glass back. "And I brought facial masks, so don't let me forget."

"Oh fun, my skin could use a little repair." Aurora set a pillow in her lap and used it to support her glass. "How's everything going at your house?"

"A gecko made its way into the bathroom last night. I'm surprised you didn't hear Camden scream all the way out here." Trinity laughed. "It was a big one too, at least six inches."

"You'd think by now he would've gotten used to the harmless little creatures." Aurora rubbed her finger on the rim of the glass. "I wonder if they have a fear-of-geckos class he can take, like immersion therapy."

Trinity threw her head back and laughed so hard she shook the couch. "I want him to get over his fear of geckos, not pass out and die." When the laughter simmered, Trinity said, "Can we talk about Gavin?"

"*You* can talk all you want about Gavin."

"Funny." Trinity flipped her long mane of hair over her shoulder and leaned forward, crossing her legs on the couch.

"Nothing to talk about. He's been a huge help with setting up the windmills. We're just about ready to get the tanks in. Our relationship is about the nonprofit organization, and while he happens to spend extra time with us, it's only because he likes to keep busy. Have you seen the news on the hurricane?"

"I saw the horrible videos of the aftermath this morning with over a foot of rainfall, but I missed the information on the storm surge height. Is he planning to go back right away?"

"Oddly enough, he seems to be avoiding any mention of it. Like something bad is attached to it, outside of the normal destruction. And he's been different since I mentioned the money to pay him."

"It's times like these that I miss Mama. We could get the truth out of her." Trinity shifted on the couch. "Are you going to keep avoiding what else I want to hear?"

"It doesn't matter. Gavin is great. He's handsome, kind, funny, and great with the girls. But . . . he's pulled away slightly since Halloween night. Like a switch turned off." Aurora's eyes traveled to the photo of Mike and the girls in a picture frame on the bookcase.

Trinity leaned forward, her hair falling around her shoulder. "You don't have to explain anything to me. I just want to see you happy again. I want to see you in love again."

Aurora reached her hand out and set it on Trinity's. "I want that so much too, regardless of Gavin—he has his own life. But how do I know when it's right for me? When will I know it's okay for the girls? Is it ever going to be okay for us?"

She could no longer make out the tan line from where her wedding ring once lived. Aurora had removed it on New Year's Eve, although it was still with her, around her neck.

"How can I push past it when I'm torn about the guilt it causes? Because saying I want to move on sounds cold and harsh."

"I'm not here to judge you; we know I'm here for wine and a mommy break." Trinity tilted her head.

"Oh, I know all about that." Aurora raised her glass and they tapped the rims.

"All joking aside, hon, only you will know when you're ready. So don't let me or anyone else in town judge your decision."

Aurora rolled her eyes. "I think Woolsey's middle name is Judge."

"Let me ask you, what do you feel guilty about with Gavin?"

"I'll stop you before you go any further. Even if I'm reading into his shift in behavior towards me, he doesn't live here. And *if* I was ready, the last thing I need is a long-distance relationship."

"Take Gavin out of the equation." Trinity shifted further back into the couch.

"Okay." Aurora pinched her eyes closed for a second before opening them. "I know something is missing in my heart, and I also know that whatever man I meet won't be able to fill the spot because it will forever belong to Mike. Is that wrong to want to be loved again but also know that it'll never be the same?"

"I think the right guy—the one you are supposed to be with—will know the importance of the girls' father as well as understand the emotions and remaining love a widow holds for their spouse." Trinity rested her hand over the top of her glass.

"Is there a rule book for this? For dating after death?"

"Yes, there are plenty of books, but you don't need a book. You're not going to be the same as the other widows, and they're not the same as you."

"We're having so much fun, the girls and I. I mean, Gavin is . . . he's becoming a good friend. And at this point, that's what I need. I needed the chance to dip my pinkie in the frosting and have a sweet little taste even if I don't get to have the entire dessert."

Trinity rested her head on the throw pillow behind her. "I think this is where I say I'll always support you and never judge you, but I shouldn't have to because you know that."

Aurora felt the lump in her throat. Inside, she battled a desire to feel whole again while she fought off the worry and guilt. If and when she became the better half of a relationship, would her fear of losing another man overwhelm her thoughts?

"Hey," Trinity said, "let's talk about something else, something happy."

"Your mom." Aurora sipped her wine. "I saw R. J. drop her off late the other night."

Trinity sat up straight. "And I saw R. J. and the judge leaving the diner this morning."

"The love triangle has been going on for a while now, maybe too long, it's crazy." Aurora stood, setting her wineglass on the coffee table. "I could use some chocolate. And there is plenty of it in the chocolate chip pumpkin cookies the girls and I made."

"Another fall bucket list item?" Trinity leaned her arm over the back of the couch.

"Yes, I worry they're starting to drive Gavin crazy with all the things they want to do with him."

"What's next on the list?"

"A bonfire with s'mores, but I told them Gavin will probably be busy." Aurora set four chewy cookies on a plate and returned to the couch. "They acted like I took their puppy away."

"You're all in a difficult spot when it comes to Gavin." Trinity held up her free hand. "Sorry! I know, change the subject. So, has my mom said anything to you about R. J.? I mean, I know she tells you more than me."

Aurora took a bite of the cookie, the pumpkin and chocolate mixed perfectly together. "Well, being right next door makes it a bit easier."

Trinity pulled a cookie off the plate and examined it before trying it. "I think R. J. simply can't decide. He's been a widow for so many years, and it's taken him a long time to open up to another woman. He's undecided because he worries about making the wrong choice, like you."

"Yeah, your mom is so adventurous, like his late wife. And the judge is witty and sharp, but I don't think she's one for much adventure."

"Do you think finding a new love and settling down is harder when you're older?"

Trinity licked her fingers and took a swig of wine. "I think when you're older, you know sooner. You get straight to the point. You know what you like and what you don't, and you have no time to waste."

"R. J. must be younger than he looks then," Aurora smirked.

# Chapter 16

## Gavin

He'd pulled out of the judge's driveway and found himself driving only a few feet to the city center's parking lot. Gavin turned the volume down on his truck's radio and stared out the windshield at the landscape in front of him. The sun had risen about thirty minutes ago, and the view of it peeking up over the rugged mountains caused a beautiful distraction.

Holding his phone horizontally, he snapped a photo through the windshield. Jesser Parish had many stunning sunrises and sunsets, but something about the vast open space surrounded by rough mountains made Arizona sparkle with a different kind of radiance. While he didn't take pictures for anything other than personal memories, this one needed to be shared with others.

Gavin had social media accounts but rarely checked them and only posted a few photos a year. Yet, his college and high school friends kept in touch through the platforms, so he remained on them.

As he pulled up his Instagram account, Gavin expected to see the devastation from those who stayed through the hurricane, capturing the aftermath. However, all his friends were posting pictures from hotels with family. Was everything still shut down? He pulled up the maps, hit traffic notifications, and zoomed in on LA 26 and LA 383 to find they were closed. He continued to move around the screen with his finger. Nearly every highway system within Louisiana had a red circle with a line through it in the state's southern region.

While he knew his skill set was needed back home, at this point, there wouldn't be any rebuilding until the waters receded and the cleanup began. The hurricane had rolled over the state only two days ago. He couldn't help thinking about what he had to lose in Jesser Parish and the reason why he wavered about his future there. He couldn't take another lost romance or destroyed home. And unfortunately, he was confident he would return home to find another disaster to rebuild.

A rapping of knuckles on the driver's side window caused Gavin to jump in his seat. Standing outside the truck was a well-dressed thin man Gavin had seen before but couldn't place.

Gavin popped the door open. "Hey, there."

"Gavin, I presume." He stuck out his hand. "Alexander."

"Alexander." Gavin shook his hand.

"I'm the librarian."

"Sorry, it took me a bit. I knew I recognized you." Gavin rested his hand on the frame of the door.

"I suppose without my face in a book it's hard to recognize me. Must be like a person out of uniform." Alexander slid his hands into his pressed navy-blue dress slacks. "Horrendous, the reason for your visit. I caught an update on the national news. Such devastation." He shook his head.

Gavin wrapped his hands on the steering wheel and gave a single nod.

"Do you know when you can return home?"

"The winds need to be less than thirty-nine miles an hour before the power crews can begin to restore them, but the water also needs to have receded. Anyone who lives in Louisiana, especially the southern part, is aware that hurricanes are a way of life there."

"We have monsoon storms here, but nothing compared to a hurricane—at least, from what I've read in books and seen on the news. I've not had the opportunity to experience one before. I suppose that's a blessing."

"Unless you're fond of super wet wind."

Alexander tilted his head as though confused by Gavin's sarcastic comment.

The scent of cow manure tickled Gavin's nose. He'd passed several areas on the drive from across the states and into New Mexico and Arizona where cows stood under shaded open-air stable structures. Thinking of Ava saying wild cows caused him to chuckle.

"Is everything alright with your truck?" Alexander asked.

"Oh yes, I pulled over to look at this view."

In front of them, State Route 287 ebbed and flowed like a well-guided river into the distance. He could also make out the roofs of the local stores and the one restaurant that flanked the sides of the road.

"I presume much different than the views of Louisiana." Alexander turned and looked in the direction of Gavin's eyeline.

"Nature has a way of showcasing such different versions of beauty."

"It takes a specific type of person, in my opinion"—Alexander gestured to his chest—"who can see the grandeur of the Southwest. There are several types of desert landscapes across the United States, Africa, and even Greenland. Are you aware Greenland is a desert? Most don't know that, yet nothing is quite the same as the Arizona desert."

"Greenland's a desert?"

"It's considered an arctic desert due to the lack of rainfall." Alexander turned back to Gavin. "Be sure and come by the library once it's open today. There's an outstanding book, *This Cold Heaven* by Gretel Ehrlich, that you might enjoy. Shall I put it on hold for you?"

"Well, I don't have a library card. I assume I would need to be a resident."

"While I am one for abiding by the law, I can make an exception for you because of your predicament and allow you to use Aurora's account."

"I . . ." He stopped himself from asking how Alexander knew he was spending time with Aurora; he knew better. Again, Woolsey was not any different than Jesser. "Thank you, Alexander."

Alexander read his wristwatch. "We open in fifty-eight minutes and close precisely at five p.m."

"I have some work to attend to today, but I'll keep it in mind."

"Have a good morning." Alexander bowed his head and pivoted, making his way back across the small parking lot.

As Gavin started his truck up, he squeezed his phone, thinking about his life back home. Jesser had many positives, but one glaring negative, and oddly enough, it wasn't devastating hurricanes. It didn't have Aurora.

# Chapter 17

## Aurora

Aurora pulled her wide brim hat tightly down over her head. Hopefully it would block some of the windburn if it picked up again today. After checking the time on the oven, she filled up several water bottles and set them inside a tiny blue cooler filled with ice. Today's high would be around eighty-seven, and with the humidity hovering around twelve percent, they would need to stay hydrated.

Even though they'd spent the last several days building the other two windmills, she couldn't wait to see Gavin the following morning. It didn't matter how much time they spent together, it never completely satisfied her need.

The sounds of crunching gravel in the driveway alerted her to Gavin's arrival. She opened the front door and found the cowboy climbing from his truck. His beard had grown out over the last few days, and Aurora had spotted a few grays weaved between the coffee-brown shade when they stood in the sunshine. As he stepped in front of her, she noticed his nose had a slight crookedness to it, and she thought it was cute; perfection was overrated.

"Exactly how many flannel shirts do you own?" Aurora shifted the weight of the cooler in her hand.

"Not enough." He smiled. "And good mornin' to you, too."

Aurora smiled. "Good morning. I packed us some water since you wanted to handle the food."

"Perfect, Lizzy sent me with fixin's for tomato sandwiches." Gavin held up a cherry-red cooler.

"I have three three-hundred-gallon galvanized tanks. I picked them up the other day in the next town over. Well"—she placed a hand on her hip—"*I* didn't actually pick them up." She pointed to them. "They're already on the flatbed to tow out there."

"I'm rather disappointed you didn't physically pick them up but glad I didn't miss your Wonder Woman strength." Gavin followed her to the 4Runner.

She peeked back over her shoulder at him. "Oh, you have jokes this morning."

"Blame Alexander. He started it."

"I highly doubt the most straight-laced man in town joked with anyone, let alone an outsider."

He stopped walking and tilted his head upward, putting a finger on his chin. "Maybe I do have jokes."

"Are they jokes if I have to figure them out? Shouldn't I just be able to laugh when appropriate?" *Stop flirting with him!* Aurora fiddled with the keys in her hand and popped the hatchback. "So, after today, the major work will be running the rest of the hoses from the windmills to the tanks. And to try and avoid the swarm of bees that will be attracted to the water."

Gavin took a step back while the hatchback rose on its own.

"So, are you ready, flannel cowboy?"

"Oh, is that my new nickname?" Gavin placed the judge's cooler into the back of the 4Runner next to Aurora's cooler. "It seems unfair that I have one and you don't."

"I'm far too wonderful to have a nickname." She watched as his eyes traveled the length of her body and then paired

90

up with her vision, his right brow raised slightly. "Well?" She tapped her boot in the dust.

"I'll come up with one before I leave."

A twitch of melancholia coursed through Aurora's body. Of course she knew Gavin would be heading home to Louisiana, but she was taken aback that acknowledging it caused her heart to ache. Nevertheless, it was a fact, and she would focus on the help he provided and how lucky she and the girls were to have the time they did have with him.

"I look forward to you never figuring out a nickname." She climbed into the driver's seat and started the engine as Gavin stood at the driver's side door.

He patted the window frame. "Meet me over at the flatbed, and I'll hook it up."

"Thank you, it was a pain to unhook, but I didn't want to try and make it through the drop-off line at school." She put the 4Runner into drive and eased it alongside Gavin until she could back it up to allow for the attachment.

Once Gavin climbed inside the vehicle, Aurora breathed in the warm scent of amber and hickory. And she was sure she'd never forget the way it relaxed her. "The girls have been talking about you nonstop."

"I'm sure we're overdue with crossin' something else off of Ava's fall bucket list." He rested his elbow on the armrest as Aurora drove them to the closest windmill.

"She wants to do a scavenger hunt, but that means we'll have to go back up north." Aurora turned the radio off.

"I had a lot of fun on our picnic hike. I can't wait to tag along."

"Really? Are you sure?"

"As sure as I like flannel, apparently."

She hummed a laugh. "How does tomorrow sound? I mean, as long as you aren't tired of me after today. I know I've taken up nearly all your time since you arrived."

"Good thing I don't look at the clock much then, isn't it?"

Aurora used her teeth to pull in her bottom lip to keep from making a noticeable blushing smile. However, it took everything she had not to crank up the air conditioner and shove her face directly onto the vent.

"I have sort of an odd request."

"Shoot," she said as she pulled up in front of the last installation site.

"I need to borrow your library card."

Aurora shut off the engine, simultaneously turning to him. "You're right, that's an odd request."

Gavin guffawed and popped open the passenger door. "I ran into Alexander, and he recommended this book on Greenland. I can read almost any book in only a few hours, so I wouldn't have it checked out but a day. It would be something to occupy my mind in the evening."

They strolled to the back of the 4Runner where the trailer held the tubs.

"Come to think of it, the girls and I need to return some books to the library. Would you mind waiting for them to tag along? They love to go, especially when the city center is decorated up, and would be disappointed if I went without them." Aurora unstrapped one side of the galvanized tubs from the flatbed while Gavin undid the other side. "Don't take this the wrong way, but why not use Lizzy's library account?"

"She doesn't have one. She only listens to audiobooks. And I guess the library doesn't carry those, thus she has no reason to get one."

Aurora placed a hand on her hip. "I'm surprised. I took her as a library fanatic. She gives off that vibe."

"Back when she babysat me, she'd read to me no matter how high the stack of books I brought her was. And I'd ask her to reread some to the point where I remember the book mysteriously disappearing, but only when she was over."

Aurora set her hands on her hips. "The girls have definitely lost a few picture books into the same mysterious void."

Gavin chuckled as they hoisted one of the tubs off the trailer and rested it just to the left of the flatbed. Taking several rest breaks, together they moved the tub to the base of the first windmill.

"Why not set the tanks up closer to your house? That way you can keep a better eye on them?"

"I want to make sure that the horses, bighorns, and deer feel safe. The last thing they need is two screaming girls running around and chasing them off with excitement. My girls aren't afraid of nature in any way. And, as you saw the other night, if they want to come close to the house, they will."

"You have bighorns here?" Gavin adjusted his cowboy hat.

"Desert bighorn sheep, they're beautiful. From what I know, they can go weeks without water, so less likely to stop by."

"I hope I get lucky and see one."

She wiped the sweat already forming and softly smiled. "Me too."

The last time they were out here, they'd run the discharge pipe and had the end resting on a concrete block to prevent it from bending. Aurora and Gavin set the tub near the location where they would drop it into the soon-to-be dugout hole. Finally, after spending a good two hours digging, the hole was ready for the tub to be lowered in. Working together, they shared glances but didn't say much of anything due to the heat and exertion of manual labor.

Once the tub was lowered, Aurora lifted the hat off her head and wiped the perspiration away with the back of her hand. "I don't know about you, but I'm more than ready for lunch." She returned the hat to her head. "Unless you want to power through and do the other tubs?"

Gavin removed his cowboy hat to reveal sweat had caused his longish brown hair to curl at the tips. While he looked attractive, she felt like a dripping mess. She worried about getting near him and hoped the breeze would work in her favor.

"No, let's rest and eat. It'll help us cool down a bit too." Gavin opened the 4Runner's back end and removed the cooler.

He pulled out the items one by one. The cooler contained bread, tomato slices, a tiny tub of mayonnaise, and a packet of salt. Aurora sat down at the edge of the 4Runner and placed a slice of bread on the top of each of their legs.

"You make a lot of sandwiches on the go, I take it?" he pointed at Aurora's knees.

"We have a lot of last-minute picnics." A wave of ambivalence washed over her, and she needed to fill the worry in her head. "You know, I've never had one of these before"—she pointed at the sandwich—"but I thought better than to ask where the rest of the stuffing was."

"Stuffing?" As Gavin sat next to her, their outer thighs, separated by their jeans, touched lightly.

"Yes, you know the fillings—lettuce, some meat, maybe cheeses," Aurora added, trying to ignore the tingling in her entire body from simply having his leg next to hers.

"Ah, stuffing, cute." Gavin opened up his water bottle and took a long sip, his Adam's apple on full display. "And you know I like my meats and cheeses. But this is supposed to be this way."

"What do you call it?" Aurora tapped her shoulder into his and noticed her feet swung like she was a kid. Feeling foolish, she quickly stopped them.

"It's a tomato and mayo sandwich." He took another bite which made nearly half the bread disappear.

Aurora held the sandwich with both hands and took a healthy bite. "Well, it is a rather delicious sandwich."

"Of course, it's nothing like what I can make back home. The tomatoes from the neighborhood garden are somethin' else."

The mention of his home instantly caused Aurora's jaw to clench, and she lowered the sandwich. "Any news from Jesser?" She hesitated with her words, acutely aware that her heart was not ready for him to leave.

Aurora watched Gavin as he stared off into the desert acreage of the Easton property in front of them. "Not much. The phone lines are a mess, and most residents still have a landline. I've not seen anything posted locally on social media from anyone in town, which makes me believe it's much worse than we thought it would be. All the posts are from residents at hotels."

"Have you ever considered moving north? So you could still be in Louisiana but less . . . in the path of the hurricanes?"

"It worked for my parents, but it's kind of all or nothing for me. Jesser is my hometown, and I've never considered living anywhere else."

"I assume it's the same for someone living in Tornado Alley."

"And we get those too." Gavin tapped Aurora with his shoulder, and instant energy returned as though he'd plugged her into a charger.

"Home is often a strong, grounded love—or at least that's how I think of it." Aurora gazed at the barely visible roofline of her home in the distance. "History connects us through roots and makes it hard to leave something so important."

Gavin nodded his head as though he was listening to a slow song's rhythm only he could hear, and Aurora wondered what he was thinking.

# Chapter 18

## Gavin

The air held the scent of moisture and foliage as Willa and Ava dashed off in front of him and Aurora on a wide path that edged the shimmering lake. As the clear water rested along the bank, they made their way farther into the shaded woods of white-barked trees with golden leaves.

"Okay, I admit, again, wow. This is stunnin'." Gavin's jaw slacked as his eyes took in the scene around him.

"It always reminds me of a screensaver or something from Pinterest." Aurora's hands were shoved into her jacket pockets, and a red scarf was wrapped loosely around her neck.

The sun's light shined off the lake, but the temperature was in the mid-fifties, making their noses a little chilly.

"I found a pine cone, Mom," Willa called from several feet ahead of him, Ava, and Aurora.

"Great, what's next on the list?" Aurora asked.

Ava removed a folded-up piece of paper from her pink coat pocket. She held it close to her face as Gavin stepped up behind her. "Look, Gavin, an acorn. We need to find an acorn."

He gave a side glance to Aurora, who was now standing on the other side of Ava, holding Willa's hand. "Acorns? In Arizona?"

"If we can find a white oak—I believe that's the tree they come from—then yes, we have acorns." Aurora's eyes squinted as though pulling the thought from the back of her mind.

He noticed whenever she needed to answer something that was from the past, she would tilt her head slightly to the left and squint while she ran her tongue over her front teeth as her upper lip plumped out. She was as full of delightful surprises as Arizona's fall was proving to be.

"Come on, Willa, let's go help Ava find an acorn," Gavin announced.

Willa reached for his hand, and he allowed her tiny fingers to wrap around his pinkie and ring finger as they headed around the north side of the lake. The sound of Aurora's footsteps echoed between the pines behind him.

"You're a plethora of information, Aurora," Gavin said over his shoulder.

"I try, but to be fair, I took a few environmental science classes in college. Unfortunately, I had no idea what I wanted to be when I grew up, so taking an array of courses for my electives caused me to graduate with extra credits. Silly, right?"

"I don't think so."

"Mike always said it was." Aurora's pace slowed, and her voice grew softer.

"And . . . why was that?" Gavin paused and glanced back over his shoulder.

Willa let go of his hand and had skipped ahead, but was still within sight.

"Because he was big on making everything count and not wasting time. Plus, I ended up becoming a stay-at-home mom and therefore never used my degree."

"None of that's true. You started a nonprofit. And being a mom is one of the most challenging jobs out there. I don't think anything you learn is ever wasted." Gavin wanted to pull her into a hug, and that want caused his arms to ache.

"Thank you." Aurora looked down as though embarrassed by his comment. "What did you do for work right out of college?"

"Same thing I do now, construction. It made logical sense to get a business degree because it would allow me to obtain some higher-up positions if I ever wanted to do something that involved less manual labor."

"Do you ever get tired of it?"

Gavin scratched at his chin. "Thankfully, no, and I know I'm lucky."

"I can say that I do love being a mom, but my mind feels like mush at times with limited adult conversations. I think that's one reason why the nonprofit is important to me."

They stepped ahead on the trail, and Gavin's heart overtook his privately wavering thoughts. "I don't want this to come off mean-spirited, but what is there to do in Woolsey? Y'all don't have much in the way of employment opportunities."

There, he'd said it or asked it—the curiosity of what might be lingered long enough.

"That's what makes Woolsey so special. People live there because they love it, because it's part of them. A few commute into Cactus City for work, and they don't mind a little driving. Don't you have to drive all over as a construction worker?"

"I try to stay local, but at times have to venture out to other parishes." His chest expanded as he took a deep breath. Lately he'd allowed his heart to ponder leaving Jesser, knowing he didn't have an answer as to the state of his hometown, and the hurt caught between his ribs.

Ava's head stretched toward the ground, inspecting the base of each tree at the edges of the path. Gavin paused and knelt next to her. Willa set her small and warm hand on his shoulder, and a memory of Jax flashed in his thoughts. It took great strength not to rub his forehead, trying to rid it of his mind. He stood up, hoping that would be enough to shake the memory.

"Look, Gavin." Willa's outstretched hand held an acorn so tiny it matched the little girl perfectly.

Just as he was about to congratulate Willa on her find, Ava crashed into his leg, hugging it. Aurora's sweater touched his arm, pressing up against him. He felt a twitch as his hand wanted to reach down to hers. Aurora smelled of sweet almonds covered in glistening sugar.

"Squirrel!" Willa cried out.

Gavin and Aurora looked where she pointed as a squirrel darted across the path, disappearing deep into the woods, traveling up a hill to the left.

"You're right." Aurora's neck craned up.

"That's a squirrel; check it off the list, Ava." Gavin kept his eyes on Aurora as his mind slipped off into his thoughts.

Her charm, her radiance, her childlike demeanor when it came to adventuring with her daughters, her drive, her heart. The only other woman he'd ever had these deep feelings for was Mila. A flood of snapshots showcasing their memories shot through him. What was he doing continuing to hang out with the Eastons? Why was he toying with the notion of giving up his life in Jesser?

"Gavin?" Aurora asked, waving her hand in front of his face. "You zoned out for a second."

He adjusted his cowboy hat, running his hand along the side of the brim. "Thank you for lettin' me tag along with you on these fall adventures. I'm havin' a great time."

She rested her hand on his arm and bit her lower lip, pulling it inward as though stopping her from saying whatever was showing concern in her eyes. "We've enjoyed having you with us. We know you won't be here much longer, but hopefully, it's been enough to take your mind off what awaits you when you return home."

A breeze picked up, rustling the leaves of the trees and causing a golden flurry of foliage to dance in the air as it drifted down, landing around them.

"There is a place only a few miles from here, and they have the best pizza." She brought her hand to her forehead. "Wait, I'm sorry. I didn't mean to assume you don't have anything better to do back in town."

"Yeah, I have so much to do, like sittin', wanderin', and then sittin' some more." Gavin chuckled. "Tell me, what makes this pizza place great? It's going to be hard to top Mammy's Pizzeria back home."

"Well, I guess you could be right." Aurora winked.

"We should go find out." Gavin followed them as they continued around the lake.

"Are you sure?" Aurora asked over her shoulder, causing her to stumble slightly. "No, pressure, honestly, we can head straight home if you'd like."

"You can't mention pizza around me and then not follow through." He stepped next to her, the girls in front of them. "I mean, cheese."

Aurora smirked. "Well, now I'm worried about it not being as good as Mammy's Pizzeria."

"Don't worry."

There was one thing that Mammy's didn't have, Aurora's company.

# Chapter 19

## Aurora

"Ava, may I please see the list?" Gavin said as Aurora merged off of I-17, taking exit 28.

She handed it up to him in the passenger seat. "What are you looking for?"

"Well, I don't think we can eat pizza if it's not on the list." Gavin looked back over his shoulder.

"Mommy!" Willa whined. "Is that true?"

"We have to stick to fall things, and I don't think there is any way that pizza can help us with the list." Gavin turned around in his seat and faced Willa and Ava.

Aurora kept her focus on the road but turned down the radio. "I think Gavin's right."

Gavin glanced over the list at the girls. "Let's see . . ." he playfully pondered, "is there anything fall-ish about pizza?"

Silence filled the 4Runner. Even Aurora had to think about it for a second.

"Pizza has red sauce. Red is a fall color," Ava stated.

"Red!" Willa cheered.

"Right, Ava." Aurora glanced into her rearview mirror to see her daughter's face.

"Yellow for the cheese," Ava said. "And brown for the crust."

"And what colors represent fall?" Gavin asked.

"Red, yellow, brown. But, Gavin, what about orange?" Ava asked.

"You don't put orange slices on your pizza?" Gavin asked.

"Gross!" Willa laughed. "No, Gavin."

"I think Gavin's right." Both of Aurora's hands gripped the wheel. "Not about the oranges, but I think three out of four colors is pretty good."

"Shall we add pizza to the list?" Gavin asked.

"Yeah!" Ava and Willa cheered.

Aurora was smitten, there was no denying it as she felt her cheeks grow rosy at Gavin's ability to help her kids learn and also laugh. And maybe, just maybe, she had learned that it was possible to find love again.

Ten minutes later, with thick gray clouds developing above, Aurora parked the 4Runner in front of the tiny ever-green-painted building that resembled a house. An array of orange, white, and speckled pumpkins lined the sides of the steps leading to the front door. A white sign in the middle of the porch's roof read, Cabin Home Pizza.

"We've been here with Daddy," Willa stated from the back seat.

The words hit Aurora in the heart, causing her chin to quiver, and she held her breath, trying to stop it. She pinched her eyes closed, hoping to escape the memory from continuing. It's not that she'd forgotten they came here as a family, it was simply that unfortunately, she couldn't get around not running into their history just about everywhere.

"Girls, let's go check out those pumpkins." Gavin's hand rested on her right shoulder for several seconds.

She moved her left hand off the steering wheel and clasped it over his.

"Come in when you're ready, and text me if you need me to come out."

She heard Gavin's door open, followed by the unbuckling of seat belts and rear doors opening and slamming closed.

As she sat alone in the 4Runner, Aurora allowed herself to cry, the pressure in her heart escaped through the tears. Yet, she was upset at herself for being emotional about a place—a silly pizza place of all things. The hike around the lake had caused Aurora to forget about her sadness. Simply being with Gavin allowed a freedom, yet, at the same time, she needed to remind herself he was not staying. He was not and would not be able to be anything more than a friend.

When she opened her tear-filled eyes, exhaustion engulfed Aurora. The restaurant appeared like a tiny cabin one would find nestled in the woods. A small plastic chef in a white hat, holding an Open sign, stood level with the porch's railing. Visions of Mike and her here danced in her mind.

Forcing herself to blink, Aurora's eyelashes stuck together with the wetness of tears. Rain drops loudly plopped against the windshield, blurring her view outside.

Aurora reached up and flipped the visor down to access the vanity mirror in order to check her makeup in it. She'd only put on a little foundation and mascara but wanted to make sure it hadn't run.

When she flicked the mirror back into place, she took a deep breath. "You can't make new memories with Mike, but you can make the most of every new memory."

Opening her driver's side door, the sky above crackled and rumbled as the raindrops intensified. She hurried up the steps and flung open the restaurant's door, causing the cow bell on the handle to bong-bong-bong.

Inside resembled a 1980s Pizza Hut, and as she wiped her boots on the entry mat that read *Have a slice day!*

Aurora ran both hands through her damp hair. When she spotted Gavin, Willa was sitting next to him in a booth with Ava across from them. Their heads were all down, coloring on the butcher-block paper lining the tables. Her hand went to her heart, and she squeezed her shirt in her grip, lowering her chin to it.

"Mommy"—Willa looked up—"come color with us."

Gavin's eyes met hers, and he mouthed, "Are you okay?"

Aurora gently smiled and nodded as she eased into the booth, sitting next to Ava. "Did you already put in the pizza order?"

"Yes, we got it with extra oranges. I hope that's okay?" Gavin said with a straight face.

Aurora busted up laughing as she picked up a blue crayon. Dang, she was going to miss him when he left.

# Chapter 20

## Gavin

Since there was not an extra car sitting in the driveway, Gavin didn't expect to see someone other than Lizzy when he opened the judge's front door.

"Hi, my apologies. I didn't mean to interrupt anythin'." Gavin shut the door behind him and shoved his truck keys into his front pocket.

On the couch, sitting relatively close together, was Lizzy and a man he recognized but couldn't place. Two tall glasses of what looked like iced tea rested before them on the coffee table's coasters.

"Nice to meet you, Gavin, I'm R. J." The man appeared to be the same age as Elizabeth, and when he stood, he showcased his striped suspenders.

Gavin shook R. J.'s hand. "Oh, you own Hammer and Nail. How are you doin'?"

"Doing well, thank you. Liz and I were just enjoying her wonderful sweet tea and some conversation." R. J. hiked his jeans at the hips as he returned to sitting on the couch.

Gavin remembered something Aurora had said about a love triangle in town having to do with Lizzy and Lillian. He wondered if this was the man involved.

"Lizzy makes the best sweet tea." Gavin headed toward the kitchen. "I think I'll grab some and take it to my room."

"How was your time with Aurora and her kids?" Elizabeth asked as he opened the refrigerator.

"Great. The lake we walked around was somethin' I didn't expect. Then we had delicious pizza and a nice surprise rainstorm made everything feel very fall-like." He removed a cup from the cupboard and poured himself a glass before returning to the living room. "The girls were so tired they napped on the way back."

"And did you drive, or Aurora?" Elizabeth wore a low-cut red wrap blouse, and her curls were controlled by a clip on each side of her head.

"Aurora." Gavin stepped closer to the hall.

"Then you napped on the way home too."

"It's possible." He tilted the glass to his lips and took a gulp.

"Hopefully, you didn't snore," Elizabeth said.

"I don't snore." Gavin stared at her in perplexity. "I don't know what you might be referring to."

"If she put up with that, she's a keeper." She picked up her glass without making eye contact with him.

Gavin smirked. "Nice to meet you, R. J."

Entering the guest room, he flipped on the light switch and shut the door. Setting his glass on the nightstand, he lowered onto the bed. Leaning back, Gavin removed his boots by pressing the toe of his right boot into the back of the left one. Then he pulled his wallet from his pocket, along with his cell phone, and tossed them on the blanket.

Laughter from the living room trickled down the hall and under his bedroom door. He leaned back against the headboard, grabbed his tea and phone, and started to type a text. He paused, erased it, then laid the phone upside down next to him.

Scratching at his head, he picked the phone back up and typed again, only to delete it. He crossed his arm over his chest, the cell in his grasp. Finally, he gave in and typed another text, hitting send before he could second-guess himself.

**Gavin: Guess who's here?**

He stared at his phone and then tossed it on the bed. *This is silly, trying to start a conversation after he'd spent the whole day with her.*

Picking up the remote off the nightstand, he clicked on the TV and began flipping through the channels. He hadn't checked the news all day since he was diligently avoiding the current state of Louisiana. Stopping on a college football game, he picked up his phone just as it alerted him to a text message.

**Aurora: Ghostbusters?**

Gavin chuckled and responded with a ghost emoji.

**Gavin: Not even close. R. J.**

**Aurora: The plot thickens.**

**Gavin: Thanks again for inviting me along today.**

**Aurora: I should be thanking you. I think you're the girls' new best friend.**

Placing his phone on his lap, he ran his hands over his cheeks, pressing against the bridge of his nose, then up to his forehead and through his hair. *Home. Home is not here.* Yet, having to remind himself of this worried him. Nothing was permanent. He was going back home soon, and once he did, this would all be a fond memory.

**Gavin: I look forward to our next bucket list adventure.**

**Aurora: Me too. . .Are you watching the Ole Miss game?**

His eyes grew wide as he glanced up at the television. *Great, she likes football.*

Looking up at the ceiling he said, "You're making this impossible."

# Chapter 21

## Aurora

Aurora cut the top off three bags of candy corn and tried her best not to roll her eyes like a teenager as she handed one bag to Willa before lifting her to the stove so she could pour it into the saucepan. Then she allowed Ava to pour the remaining two bags in while standing on a step stool she'd moved in front of the stove. Next, Aurora lowered Willa to the floor, and Ava helped stir the mixture as Aurora added heavy cream.

Delight etched across Aurora's face when she glanced around the kitchen at the scene—Gavin, sitting on a barstool in front of the island. Willa at her legs, happily chattering about making ice cream. Ava standing at the stove, stirring the melting candy. Joy coursed through her veins. If only this would last . . . forever. But Aurora knew forever was impossible.

"Once we get this in the freezer to chill, we can head to the library." Aurora used her fingers to brush Willa's hair off her cheek as she hugged her mom's legs. "Although, we can save time and just pour this right into the trash."

Gavin held his hands up in defense. "It's not my fault the girls won the coin toss and your pumpkin ice cream lost to my experimental candy corn ice cream."

"Mommy?" Ava asked as she stirred. "Can we put the picture of us in a frame? Like Dad's pictures?"

Her breath caught, and she placed her hand on her throat to remind herself to swallow.

"Mom, please?" Ava didn't turn around.

Aurora blinked. "Of course. If you want to, we can pick one out and print it."

Gavin cleared his throat and said quietly, "Should I leave?" He motioned with this thumb toward the front door.

Aurora shook her head but was conflicted. Uncertainty zipped through her. "Ava, you'll need to ask Gavin if it's okay to have a photo of him out."

Ava stepped off her stool and went over to him. She set her hand low on his back and patted it like an adult would to a child. "It's okay, right, Gavin?"

Emotions drained from Aurora's body as she laughed at the cute affection Ava showed for him, the way she mirrored things she did with them when asking questions and requesting for them to complete tasks. Often, she set a hand on their shoulder or back to make sure they were paying attention.

Gavin looked at Ava and then at her. "It's okay with me."

"See, Mom." Ava set her hands on her hips before spinning and returning to the stove to stir the liquid.

"Can I speak with you?" He pointed to the hall just outside of the kitchen wall.

Aurora pulled the corner of her lip in with her top teeth and followed him out of the room. They faced each other as she brought her arm to the top of her head and rested it there before pressing her palm onto her forehead.

"Are you okay?" He reached his hands out and wrapped his fingers around her biceps.

His touch sent aftershocks of sensations through her, and tears instantly formed in her eyes. She leaned forward, and he moved his arms, wrapping them around her as she wept. Aurora's tears mixed with the cedar scent on his cottony flannel shirt. Gavin didn't say anything as he held her, and even though she could stand, it was as if he kept her from falling.

"I'm sorry," she mumbled into his shirt. As she pushed herself off his firm chest, Aurora wiped her tears. "I'm happy. I know this sounds weird, but Ava wanting something new, wanting to be . . ." She couldn't say it, it was far too forward, not to mention impossible. But everything that was happening felt so utterly perfect it scared her.

Gavin would be leaving in a few days, and she wanted to hold on to their moments, give her girls every memory they could make with a great male role model. Not a replacement. At the same time, Aurora worried about the girls growing attached to someone who was leaving.

"Mom!" Ava yelled. "It's melted."

Aurora finished wiping her tears dry and placed her hand on Gavin's arms for a few seconds before entering the kitchen and going over to the stove.

"It looks good. Thanks for being my helper." She kissed the top of Ava's head.

After her daughter climbed down, Aurora slid the stool out of the way and shut off the burner.

"Mom, can I pick the picture?" Ava grabbed up her mom's cell phone off the counter.

Aurora held out her hand, and Ava placed the cell in her palm so she could unlock the phone before handing it back. Then she poured the melted mixture into a bowl to cool before pouring it into the ice cream machine. She caught Gavin looking for something out of the corner of her eye and turned in his direction.

His eyes darted around the room. "Where's Willa?"

"She was just here." Aurora set the saucepan in the sink to soak and walked around the island. "Willa? Ava, would you go see if your sister is upstairs, please?"

Her daughter took the cell phone with her as she skipped down the hall. Aurora checked the laundry room downstairs and the bathroom before making her way to the end of the steps. Gavin stood behind her as they looked up to the open banister, waiting for a response.

Ava appeared, casually holding the railing as she walked down the steps. "She's not up there," she said unfazed.

Worry eased through Aurora, and by the time she entered the kitchen, Gavin was at the French doors. "She must have gone outside." His words were edged with anxiety and stern-sounding as they came from his lips.

Aurora hurried over as they both exited the French doors together and spilled out onto the patio in the backyard. "Willa!" Aurora called. "I'm sure she's around here someplace. It's not like her to wander off."

"Does she have a favorite spot?" Gavin peered behind two mesquite trees, his movements jerky. "Willa!"

Aurora put her hand to her forehead to block the glare of the sun so she could see farther out onto the property.

Gavin cupped his hands around his mouth. "Willa!" he wailed.

"It's okay, we'll find her," Aurora reassured him, puzzled by his instant panic; he didn't seem like the type to worry. "It's Woolsey; even if she got lost, someone will find her."

"There are dangers in the desert which could harm her." The muscles in Gavin's face and neck stiffened.

Aurora checked the gazebo, but it was empty. "Hmm." Her mind whirred in thoughts. Where could her daughter have gone? She definitely wasn't as rattled as Gavin, though she could appreciate his concern. He jogged past her, heading toward the 4Runner and his truck.

Then she remembered the open-air hangar, where the crop duster used to be parked. Willa loved it there because it had a concrete slab, and she could draw with her chalk in the shade.

"I think I know where she might be," she called to Gavin, who jogged back over.

There was fear in his eyes, and his forehead creased as he grabbed her hand. "Where?"

Aurora scrunched her eyes, drawing her brows down, and pointed towards the hangar only about a thousand feet away. He yanked her forward, not releasing her hand, and she moved her feet as fast as she could to keep up with his wide stride.

"It's the desert. How can she wander off? Especially alone. It's not safe."

"It's okay. It's fall. A lot of harmful creatures are hiding," she reassured him, perplexed.

"There are other dangers to a young child, Aurora," Gavin hissed at her before bellowing, "Willa!"

Taken by surprise at Gavin's roughness, she yanked her hand from his as they approached the hangar.

There, sitting on her knees, Willa clutched a chunk of pink chalk in her tiny hand. Aurora watched as Gavin halted in front of her and knelt, resting his knees on the concrete below. He set his hand on Willa's back, and she looked up at him.

"Gavin, look!" She pointed at the art she'd drawn in front of her.

"Willa, honey, what has Mommy said about leaving without telling me? You know you need to have a parent with you." Aurora squatted next to Gavin and pushed her daughter's hair out of her face. Utterly unaware of how terrified a man they'd only spent a short time with had been only a few minutes ago at the idea of her being missing, Willa continued her drawing.

"Sorry, Mommy."

"Please put the chalk down and look at me." Willa did as she was told. "You worried Gavin and me very much. I need you to promise me you won't do that again." Aurora stood.

"Prom-miss."

Ava came running up to the edge of the hangar. "Is she in trouble?"

"Ava, not now. Please take your sister and go get ready for the library," Aurora said as the breeze picked up and the autumn air smelled of blooming oleanders.

Once the girls were heading back and out of earshot, Aurora folded her arms over her chest. "I didn't appreciate being snapped at about my knowledge of what is safe and unsafe with regards to my parenting skills."

Gavin shoved his hands into his jean pockets. "I apologize for that. I didn't mean it as it sounded."

"Do you want to tell me what's really going on?" Aurora sighed.

Gavin's vision traveled in slow motion to the ground and then back up, finally meeting her eyes. She could tell he was trying to say something. His mouth opened, the words possibly caught before they could escape. And Aurora knew when a memory caused someone to go silent.

Taking two steps forward, she reached out and took a hold of his hand. Right now might not be the best time to discover what worried Gavin's heart, but she'd find out when he was ready to talk about it. "Come on, let's go to the library."

# Chapter 22

## Gavin

Leaning over the bathroom sink at the city center, Gavin splashed water on his face. After being rattled by Willa's short-lived disappearance, he needed to regain his focus. And snapping at Aurora had been wrong, but he didn't know how it happened. He wished there was a way to erase the incident from both their minds. Allowing memories to control his emotions was not something he ever wanted.

Drying his face with a paper towel from the dispenser, he studied himself in the mirror. Only he didn't see himself, he saw Jax's face. The face of a sweet boy. Then he saw Mila's face.

*Move on! They're gone! Get a grip!*

Gavin would forever remember the four-year-old's grin, his adventurous spirit. And the twinkle in Mila's eyes and generosity in her smile would stay with him always. That same courage and generosity sadly led to the worst day of Gavin's life. Lives Gavin should've been able to save. If only.

Redirecting his focus to the present, Gavin opened the bathroom door and entered the hall. As he searched for the girls, he was caught off guard when a familiar person walked past him.

"Gavin!" Camden declared, stopping and turning around at the harvest-decorated pillar in the middle of the city center's main entrance. Faux orange and red maple leaves were wrapped around the structure along with glowing acorn lights. A giant poster stuck to a nearby wall read:

**Fall Fun Day!**
**Potato Sack Races, Apple Bobbing,**
**and Horseshoe Tournament** – Vendor Booths Available

In Camden's arms was a girl about two years old. "I was wondering when I might run into you."

"And this must be Jolie." Gavin smiled at the toddler wearing a pair of jean shorts, tiny tan cowboy boots, and a yellow T-shirt.

At the sound of her name, Jolie buried her face into her dad's shirt.

"Say hi to Gavin," Camden coaxed his daughter.

Jolie gave a wave but stayed buried in the safety of her dad's button-down.

"I'd figured you would've been at the Halloween house." Gavin shifted in his boots.

"They should make Halloween fall on the last Saturday of the month every year, like Thanksgiving is always on a Thursday. But I'm not sure who's in charge of deciding that." Camden chuckled and switched Jolie to his left hip. "How long are you in town for?"

"Only a few more days. Not one hundred percent sure. According to news sources, the water levels are still rather high. But now that I know about this Fall Fun Day"—he pointed at the sign—"I have to stay."

"Ah yes, it's entertaining and puts you in a festive mood—but it's dusty." Camden attempted to set Jolie down on the ground, but she latched on like a monkey to a tree branch.

"Daddy," she whined.

"Before you leave we should get Trinity's mom to watch the kids and we can catch up over dinner."

"That would be good. Let's make it happen," Gavin said.

Honestly, he was a bit surprised by the invitation. He figured the awkward night of wine with Trinity and him after they'd gone horseback riding had put the nail in their friendship coffin. But then again, at that time, Camden and Trinity's marriage hovered on divorce and probably caused his jealousy to rage.

"Perfect, I'll let Trinity know," Camden said. "I need to get home. She's making some new cookies for her company, and I'd hate to miss out on testing them while they're still warm from the oven."

"Lizzy mentioned how well her small baking company is goin'."

"Yes, it's been more profitable than we ever imagined. Be sure we get you some cookies before you leave. Or at least to take with you for the long drive home."

"I definitely won't leave town without them." Gavin smiled as though he could already taste them. "We'll meet up soon."

Camden gave a wave as he turned and headed for the main doors of the city center with Jolie on one hip.

Gavin made his way to the open library doors, directed by a large canvas Fall Into a Great Book sign with painted gourds and pumpkins. Stepping through the doors, he spotted Aurora and the girls in the children's section off to the left. The area was decorated with a bold rug in fun primary colors for what must be story time, a table with four tiny chairs, and low shelves perfect for children to access books easily.

"Hello, Gavin. I've set your Greenland book aside," Alexander announced from behind a mahogany desk near the entrance.

"Thanks, I appreciate it," Gavin mentioned.

Classic and traditional fall décor spread throughout the library, from orange pumpkins on the tops of bookshelves to cornucopias full of different sizes and shapes of gourds. He met up with Aurora as she sat in a nearby chair, allowing the girls to explore the bookshelves.

"Can I ask you about earlier?" She leaned forward over the two books she had on her lap, reminding him of a teacher ready to start circle time. "Willa running off seemed to rattle you pretty badly."

"It brought up a . . . bad memory. One I've wanted desperately to erase for a while now." He focused on the pattern of his shirt. "Yet, it reminded me I don't deserve . . ."

"Don't deserve what?" She continued to lean forward over the books. "What are you talking about?"

"It's a— It's not a happy story."

"If anyone can understand unhappiness and unfairness, it's me." Aurora leaned back into the chair and rested her hands on top of the books in her lap.

"I'm sorry I didn't mean to diminish the loss of your husband." Gavin shifted on the chair that was far too small for his frame and placed his elbows on his knees.

She shook her head. "It was nice to see how concerned you were for Willa's safety. It meant a lot to me. But at the same time, I'm sorry it brought up a bad memory. So if you need to talk about it, I'm here to listen."

He wasn't ready to talk about it. He never wanted to talk about it, but he appreciated her support. "Thank you, Aurora."

She gave a disapproving frown but something over his shoulder caught her attention, and her eyes appeared to perk up. "Hey, look who's over there." Aurora motioned with her head.

Gavin eased to his right and glanced behind him to spot R. J. flipping through a book before he put it back and removed another one from the shelf.

Her hand tapped on the top of his wrist, and he turned back around. "He's in the romance section," she whispered.

As he crossed his arms over his chest, Gavin's lips went in a straight line. "Men can read romance novels."

Aurora waved her hand at him. "I know. That wasn't why I said that. Lillian loves romance books, and my guess is he's trying to woo her by reading something she loves so they can discuss it."

"*Woo?*"

"You've never done something to impress—*woo*—a woman before?" Aurora leaned forward and tilted her head to the left.

"This feels like a trap. Is this a trap?" He watched the side of Aurora's lip twitch up enough for a dimple to appear in her right cheek.

She squinted and fanned one of the books in front of her fluttering her eyelashes. "Fine, don't tell me how much you love a thick romance novel."

Just as a grin was about to form on his mouth, Gavin's lips gaped open. "Wait a minute, R. J. was over at Lizzy's the other night."

"He's been over at Lillian's too, later in the night. I honestly think he's torn. R. J.'s been great friends with Lillian for years, and the judge moving here threw his heart for a decisional loop. I don't think he wants to hurt either woman."

"How long does it take to decide who he loves?" Gavin watched R. J. pull out another book from the shelf.

"I think it's sweet. It shows he cares enough not to hurt either one of them."

She had a point, a good point. There was never a reason to hurt someone's feelings, but R. J. had to be doing damage to his own heart by not being able to fully commit to being in love.

Willa came hopping over and handed Gavin a picture book. "Can you come and read this to me? It's a book about autumn—the season, not the girl in my class."

Before he could answer, Willa had left the book in his lap. He stood and followed her towards the other end of the children's area. Willa pulled out the chair at the small table where Ava was with a beginner's chapter book.

He attempted to sit in the tiny chair next to Willa, but his adult bottom didn't fit. Somehow these chairs were smaller than the already miniature chair he'd been sitting in moments ago. When he looked over at Aurora, she was covering her mouth, no doubt laughing.

"Gavin, please sit down," Willa instructed.

He looked left and right, trying to see what else might be available for him to sit on. Nothing. Instead, Gavin lowered himself onto the floor next to the table and crossed his legs. He was tall enough that his chest came up to the table's top, but his arms were at a poor angle to flip the pages of a book. At the current angle, he looked like a tyrannosaurus trying to read a book. But Willa didn't seem to mind as long as he kept reading; she leaned forward in her chair, hovering over the book.

Once he finished the story, Willa had another book ready and slid it his way like a person trying to hand off a tip to the hostess for a better table at a restaurant.

"Willa, please ask Gavin before you force him to read to you." Aurora came up to the table, pulled out a chair, and sat down across from him. She was clearly able to fit somewhat better on the child-size chairs.

"Can you please read this to me?" Willa tapped the book's cover with her fingers.

"Of course," Gavin chimed.

He opened another autumn-themed hardcover book. With the turn of each page, his vision went to Aurora, who remained seated across from him, her hands folded together and her chin resting on them. When the story ended, he closed the book and arched his back.

"Come on, girls. I think Gavin deserves a home-cooked meal. That is, unless he has plans for tonight?" Aurora stood and pushed the tiny chair in and walked around the table to his side.

"No plans. Say, when's that Fall Fun Day?" Gavin pointed toward the exit of the library. "I saw a banner for it outside the bathroom."

"In two weeks. They always have it the weekend before Thanksgiving."

He used the table as leverage and stood up, ending up closer to Aurora than he realized he'd be.

"I don't think I'll still be here." His voice was a near whisper.

For half a second, his eyes drifted closed as Aurora's signature scent of vanilla and brown sugar warmed his nose. The sound of her sighing deeply seemed to travel to his bones.

"That's a shame," Aurora breathed.

"However, I'd be delighted to join you tonight."

She took a step forward, and his heart raced. "I figured you'd be tired of us by now."

"Never." He barely shook his head. "This natural disaster has a serious perk."

Aurora lowered her head, but he caught her blush just before she did.

# Chapter 23

## Aurora

Aurora unlocked the living room's French doors and, with Gavin on her heels, the two snuck down the back porch and across the yard to the gazebo. The evening breeze held the scent of orange and lemon tree blossoms from Lillian's yard. Edison lights dripped down from the ceiling, providing the perfect warm glow against the blackened star-filled sky. They each held a fall-themed stemless wineglass in their hand as they sat opposite each other. Hers proclaimed she was *grateful for fall weather and ALL the wine* while his boasted *I'm only here for the wine and pumpkin pie.*

The merlot was the perfect complement to the new chicken lasagna she'd made for dinner, a recipe she snatched out of the back of the novel she was currently reading, *Grounded in July*. The wine was a dark-berry flavor mixed with hints of vanilla and mocha.

"Ava's fall bucket list is almost complete," Aurora mentioned. "I appreciate you participating and being so kind to the girls. But I'm sure you'll be glad to be home and have your life back to its regularly scheduled programming."

"Scheduled programming isn't all it's cracked up to be. The good thing about driving is I can leave whenever. I'm not tied to a plane ticket." Gavin held his glass in one hand, resting it on his knee.

She knew she couldn't ask him to stay, but Aurora wanted to. Being in his company brought about a sense of peace and coziness, like a warm-from-the-dryer blanket. She and the girls had quickly grown attached, but the last thing any of them needed was another heartbreak.

"Whatever happened to your crop duster?" He pointed with his wineglass at the empty hangar.

"I didn't feel safe taking it up after Mike passed. I couldn't leave the girls, and while I could bring them with me, I worried about something going wrong. Suddenly everything became hypersensitive. If something happens to me, the girls would be left all alone."

"I can understand that." He took a long sip of wine. "You should be proud of all you've managed as a single parent. The house alone is an enormous upkeep."

She watched Gavin's face, almost staring through it. Being outside, enjoying the cool seventy-degree night with a perfect glass of wine and company gave her comforting fuzzies. The feeling of hope and the delight of happiness was a dream she didn't want to wake up from.

"If you need any help, I'd be happy to assist before I have to leave."

"No, you've already done more than enough. Without you, I wouldn't have been able to get the windmills built and the water going." A part of her wondered if the house looked disheveled to everyone but her. Sure, she'd pushed a few things to the back burner, but it wasn't that bad, was it?

"Do you have plans for tomorrow?" she asked.

"What do you have in mind? Do you have a hot date with a paint roller?"

"No." Her eyes squinted, wondering if maybe she did need to make a home fixer-upper list. "About once a week, I go out and check the abandoned water tanks in the area. There are plenty of dried-up holding tanks, and thanks to people throwing trash in them, they can attract wildlife."

"And they can't walk in and out on their own?" Gavin put his wineglass to his lips.

"Most of them are small, like the ones we're putting in, but there are a few concrete ones that are fairly deep. Every once in a while, a coyote smells something yummy and manages to jump in but can't get back out."

"And the Arizona Game and Fish doesn't put anything over them to prevent that?"

"A few do." Aurora crossed her legs. "But overall they're so underfunded. Limited staff and time to do the maintenance needed for current windmills, wildlife preservation, and law enforcement."

"So you take it upon yourself to rescue these animals if they're in there?"

"Luckily, it's only been a handful, but a handful too many in my book. And it's enough to keep checking every week. Especially in the summer."

"I don't think you needed to dress up as Wonder Woman for Halloween. You're already wearing the costume every day."

If the wine hadn't gotten to her cheeks yet, his comment did. Thankfully the glow of the lights didn't only hide imperfections.

"Thank you," she whispered and tucked her hair behind her ear. "I feel like my girls, hogging all of our conversations. Tell me more about you."

Gavin fidgeted in his spot on the bench. "Not too much to say."

She shifted her legs and took a long sip of merlot, desperate to know the story that caused the fear in him with Willa today; however, she didn't want to push. "What got you started in construction?"

"My pa and pawpaw. Both worked construction, my pa was a roofer, and my pawpaw was a journeyman electrician. I got into carpentry and decided on residential carpentry because it allowed me to utilize more detailed skills. Restoration has always been a passion of mine since I was a little tike. I would wander the roads of Jesser, very Huck Finn style, and find abandoned houses so I could explore and take in the layout and design. Basically whatever else I could muster up to get myself in trouble. And Louisiana has more than its fair share of history and trouble to find in homes."

"I'm so fascinated by historical architecture, mostly Southern styles, but my family's roots are there, so that could easily explain it."

"Does that mean you've been to the South, just not Louisiana?"

"Yes, once to Georgia, back when I was a teenager. Of course, I'm sure age affects how you view the area."

"Growin' up there gives a different perspective than visitin'." Gavin adjusted an outdoor pillow behind his back. "It's soaked in your bones like a chicken in a pot of boilin' water."

"You must stay busy year-round and more so during a bad hurricane season, helping residents repair their homes." Aurora's comment caused her to think about him in a white T-shirt hanging drywall, his biceps peeking out. Tingles traveled through her chest as the heat of the daydream reached her ears.

"Yes, and no. Most in Jesser don't have the income to fix what's needed after a storm, and they go without. It's usually the nearby counties who have residents that can afford the repairs."

"Doesn't insurance cover the damage?"

"Sure, if the homeowner has it."

Her mouth formed the shape of an O. Aurora lowered her wineglass, looking down upon it. Never once did she have to worry about money or having insurance—before or after losing Mike—and the reminder that she was privileged and fortunate stung like a paper cut.

She glanced up at the moon, examining the gray splotches. "I don't want you to take this the wrong way, but isn't it hard to live someplace that's always in a danger zone?"

"Are you going to sing the theme song from *Top Gun?*" The corners of his mouth rose into a smile.

She giggled and covered her mouth.

"I hear what you're sayin'. But home is home." He eyed the two-story house over her shoulder. "Think about you, you'll never leave this place. It's home, it's hot in the summer and dusty as all get-out, but it's your home. Your family history might be in the South, but your roots were planted here. The same rings true for me. Hurricanes or not, Jesser is home."

His words were spot on, and they echoed through her memories of childhood. No matter what happened in life, she knew deep down inside she could never leave Woolsey, and unfortunately, she knew Gavin would never leave Jesser Parish—they couldn't have a relationship. The knowledge caused a push-pull reaction inside of her. She also knew she wouldn't have to worry anymore about if she was doing a disservice to her late husband by continuing to entertain such a notion. But it didn't stop her from wanting to stand, walk over to Gavin, and curl up next to him.

"Are you okay?" Gavin asked, his head tilted slightly to the right.

"Sorry, yeah." She waved him off and brought her wineglass to her lips. "So, tomorrow, after we get the hoses set on the tanks, we can go do my weekly rounds?"

Headlights turned off the main road, and the low rumble of an engine grew closer. She instantly noted it was R. J.'s truck. The exhaust spat and sputtered as it drove closer.

"Absolutely," Gavin mumbled as he turned toward the noise.

She squatted down, grabbing at Gavin's arm to get him to do the same.

"What's happening?" He got to his knees, the wine splashing over the top of the glass.

"It's R. J." Aurora pointed as the truck slowly rolled by as though trying to tiptoe past her house. "At this angle, he can't see us from the road."

"Oh, it's late. Sounds suspicious."

"You're here *this* late."

Gavin's face was utterly close to hers, and Aurora held her breath. They each had a hand on their wineglass and the other pressed onto the concrete floor. They faced each other as though they were auditioning for a familiar scene in *Dirty Dancing*. And while she didn't know what Gavin was thinking, she knew exactly what *she* was thinking.

He set his wineglass down next to his knee, reached out, and as Gavin's skin made contact with her cheek, she shut her eyes. Then, balancing herself on her knees, she reached her free hand up, placing it over Gavin's hand to keep it from moving.

She had no idea how long the moment lasted, a few seconds or a few minutes. But when she opened her eyes, Gavin's hand slipped from under hers. "I should probably go." He stood up and held out his hand to help her to her feet.

"Yeah, it's getting late." She sighed. "And we have another big day tomorrow."

"Thanks for dinner and the wine and . . . the company." He handed over his half-full glass.

She took it and glanced at both the glasses before looking up at him. "You're okay to drive, right?"

"Yes." He stepped backward out of the gazebo and paused. Taking two steps after him, Aurora was again, less than a foot from Gavin.

Out of the bottom of her eye, she caught his hand moving near her waist, only for him to pull it back. "I'll see you tomorrow."

He took a few more steps backward, then turned and made his way to the truck. Aurora leaned against the gazebo's support beam as Gavin opened the driver's side door and stood there. Not getting in, but not turning around.

Every muscle in her body stiffened as her heart pounded. Then, Gavin climbed into his truck and shut the door.

He rolled down the window and gave a wave before turning onto the road heading towards the highway. Aurora waved back with his glass in the air, and then she downed the last of her wine before dragging herself back inside.

# Chapter 24

## Gavin

His palms remained warm and sweat stuck his hand to the steering wheel as he turned onto the road leading to the judge's house. Gavin had come close to kissing Aurora. Too close. The way they were like two deer in a standoff on the floor of the gazebo.

As he pulled into Lizzy's driveway and shut off the engine, Gavin tried to shake Aurora from his mind, but it was stuck like gum. He still felt her cheek in the palm of his hand, and he took his thumb and pressed it into the skin, needing to erase it.

Trying to rationalize his feelings, Gavin reminded himself that the gazebo's Edison lights make everything look perfect in the dark of the night. He should know. He'd wired at least a hundred sets over the last year. But as he quietly shut the driver's side door, he knew darn well that Aurora was beautiful from any perspective.

Reaching the front porch, he removed his boots, unlocked the door, and tiptoed through the living room.

"Late night?" Elizabeth leaned against her bedroom door as he attempted to sneak into her house.

"Dang it. How do you keep doin' this?" He froze. "Did I wake you?"

She waved him off and clicked on the hall light as she made her way past him and into the kitchen. "No, but your timin' is perfect."

"For?" He followed her, boots still clutched in his hand.

"A nightcap and bread puddin'." She removed two dessert plates from the cupboard and snatched the bottle of bourbon from the back of the counter.

Gavin took two mason jar glasses from the cupboard and pulled out Lizzy's chair as she sat down, a large wooden spoon in hand.

After serving herself and Gavin, she took the glass of bourbon he'd poured and held it up. "To Mama."

Gavin took his glass, two fingers full, and clanked it against hers. "Miss you, Mama."

"Things seem to be goin' well between you and the Easton girls."

"Is that supposed to mean somethin'?" Gavin allowed the bourbon to settle.

Elizabeth cocked her head. "Yes, it is."

"I should know better by now." Gavin shoved his fork into the bready goodness.

"So you should." She sipped her bourbon. "What do you plan to do about it?"

Gavin removed his cowboy hat and set it on the table. "Nothin'. Her home is here, and my home is there. In fact, we spoke about that tonight. Not to mention that we aren't in a relationship. She isn't over her husband. And I respect that because I'm not sure I would be either." He didn't want or need to mention Mila and Jax.

"But there is somethin' there, a connection?"

The bread pudding tasted sweet on his tongue as he took another bite, thinking about his answer. Surely he wasn't going to tell Lizzy how wanted to run back to Aurora after he'd made it to his truck. How he'd almost turned around in the driveway. How when he'd closed his eyes tonight, for the first time in years, the only thing he saw was Aurora staring back at him.

Gavin leaned back into the chair but kept the fork in his grip. "Yes, but I'm headin' back home in a few days. The water is finally receding, and I need to find out what I have to fix."

"I suppose your mind is made up then." She rested her posture and crossed her arms.

"You know I can't move out of Jesser Parish. My job is there. My life is there. You're bettin' on a relationship that isn't a reality."

"But I'm never wrong. Even Mama could attest to that." She gazed up towards the ceiling. "You know some people look at fall as the start of the end, the sunlight growin' shorter, and foliage changin' and driftin' from the branches, leavin' them bare. And it takes time. It can never be rushed or happen any other time but in the time that Mother Nature has deemed fittin'. Even in January, when winter is in full swing, there is a sense of hope because it's a new year, a new beginnin'. But fall, fall is the perfect time to make changes and prepare ourselves for the new year."

"Maybe fall isn't about that at all. Maybe those leaves are getting' rid of the baggage, the sadness, firmin' up their stature to create the beauty of new growth right where they already are." Gavin stared at the glass on the table before looking at Lizzy. And when he did, she had a smile creasing ever so slightly.

"Which they can't do without losin' it all first." Lizzy rested the fork on her empty bread pudding plate.

*Two could play at this game.* Gavin cleared his throat. "What's the status of your relationship with R. J.?"

"I'm not sure what you're referring to." She tilted her head back and drained the last of the bourbon in her glass.

132

"Well, don't be pitchin' a hissy fit now. I see you with R. J. and how you're grinnin' like a possum eatin' a sweet tater." Gavin twisted the lid off the bottle of bourbon on the table between them and poured another two fingers' worth into each glass.

Lizzy took the cup in both hands and stared into it. "I enjoy his company, but he's not ready to commit. After all this time I'm not sure if he ever will be."

"Does that mean you'll keep waitin' to see if he does?"

"I'd rule him in contempt of court if I could. Lillian holds an important spot in his heart, not to mention a longtime friendship. Yet that dang man keeps pullin' me in like catfish on a line."

He rubbed his fingers over the smooth surface of the wooden table. "It appears we are both preparin' for a pivotal fall."

# Chapter 25

## Aurora

Aurora stood at the sink, washing the two empty wineglasses. The light over the stove provided an amber glow against the cold white of the kitchen. With a soapy sponge, she cleaned the fingerprints from the glasses before running them under the water and resting them on the small dish strainer on the edge of the sink to dry.

She took a pumpkin-themed dish towel and wiped her hands off as she peered out the kitchen's window. The gazebo was visible from the sink, and Aurora locked her eyes on it, envisioning what had recently played out between her and Gavin.

The desire to grab hold of his shirt and pull him close still vibrated under her fingers. She missed partnership and the passion of a relationship. She missed being needed and wanted. She missed being in love.

A woman's face appeared in the window with a smile and a quick wave, blocking her view of the gazebo and shattering her reverie. Aurora nearly jumped out of her skin before realizing it was Lillian.

Opening the right French door, Aurora's hand remained on her chest, trying to calm her heartbeat down.

"So sorry to startle you, honey." Lillian held up a bottle of wine. "I saw your light was on and needed someone to talk to."

Aurora stepped aside and motioned for her neighbor to come in.

"I know I could use some and figured you might like to join me." Lillian held the bottle in Aurora's direction.

"Oh, this isn't one that Charlie carries." Aurora took the bottle and headed to get the two glasses drying in the rack.

Lillian remained near the French doors. "It was a gift."

Removing the cork, Aurora looked over her shoulder. "Please sit, relax. But you must tell me—a gift from whom? Could it be R. J.?"

"R. J. thinks good wine comes from the gas station and contains the word *berry*." Lillian sank onto the couch.

Aurora's nose scrunched up at the thought of such wine as she handed a glass to Lillian and took a seat next to her on the couch.

"But I saw R. J.'s truck a little bit ago." Aurora took a long sip of the merlot-cabernet mix.

"You must have missed it leaving a minute later."

Aurora slid the blanket off the back of the couch and draped it over her lap. "I guess I did. So, spill."

Lillian took a drink of wine and then lowered the glass near her knee. "I love R. J. I love his company and being his friend. Yet, being friends with him, us being friends, is all we'll ever be. And we both want it that way. I think from the outside looking in it appears to be something more."

"I have to say I'm a bit surprised." Instinctively, Aurora pouted.

"So were we." Lillian laughed. "I think we hoped it would eventually turn into something more after all these years.

Instead, it's been very *When Harry Met Sally*, minus several scenes and the ending."

Aurora leaned forward. "But what was he doing tonight?"

Lillian waved her hand in a never mind motion. "Oh, he asked me to make a special dessert for tomorrow. He's going to ask the judge to, well, as he put it, 'go steady with him.'"

"That's sweet and rather old-fashioned, how very R. J."

"He's taking her on a picnic and has the deli at the Shop and Save making the main course, and my dessert will be the final touch for when he asks her."

"I'm excited for them"—Aurora reached her hand out and squeezed Lillian's arm—"but what about you? I hate you being all alone over there."

"I could say the same for you, honey."

"I'm not alone."

"Last I checked you aren't living in *The Notebook*."

"Thank goodness. There was a lot of arguing in that movie."

Lillian nodded with a laugh. "I've seen the truck with the Louisiana plates here."

"He's only helping me set up the windmills." Aurora sucked in her breath. "And has been nice enough to spend time with the girls and me. But it's because he has nothing else to do in this town."

"There will be many more windmills all over the state for him to help you with."

"Let's not jump the rattlesnake yet."

"Okay, I won't say anymore." Lillian crossed her ankles at her hot-pink Converse.

"Thank you. So, let's talk about you. If it's not R. J. then . . .?"

"You can't tell Trinity . . ." She tapped the sides of her Converse together. "I started chatting with a guy . . . online."

"Online?" Aurora brought her knees to her chin and wrapped her free arm around her legs. "Tell me more, please. I promise I won't say a word."

Lillian raised her eyebrow, and glared, giving her a side-eye. "You mean like when you promised not to tell Trin about her surprise party?"

"That was different. If I hadn't told her, she would've shown up in a nighty."

"Fair, okay. I guess it would be nice to talk with someone about it. Someone who understands what dating entails nowadays. It's so different from when I was in my twenties."

"Who's the guy?" Aurora was grateful for the distraction.

"He has a fake name or computer name. I'm not sure of the term, but we both do. I'm Desert Girl, and he's Desert Guy."

"Well, isn't that a perfect match right there. Does that mean he lives here?"

"He didn't say exactly where he lives, just in a small town. We're taking it slow and don't want to allow ourselves to learn too much that might harm our privacy until we're ready."

"And what does he do for a living? What do you talk about?"

"It's all typing, very *You've Got Mail*, so I haven't heard his voice. But he owns his own business, and he seems to love what he does. His hours are kind of irregular, so we usually only get a chance to chat late at night."

"How cool would it be if this is a love match, and he lives in Woolsey?"

"That's impossible. We know everyone here."

"And there are several single men." Aurora sipped her wine.

"And one is seventy-three."

"But the other one is not." Aurora winked. "Come to think of it, he's only a few years older than you."

"It's not Charlie Tow. He doesn't own a computer. Not to mention he's never shown any interest in me. The only thing he shows an interest in is produce and weekly sale stickers."

Aurora nearly choked on her wine as she laughed and covered her mouth.

"Sure, Charlie's cute. But it's a one-in-a-million chance it's someone in Woolsey. And one in a trillion that it's Charlie." Lillian gazed off as though catching sight of a daydream.

"That's still a chance."

# Chapter 26

## Gavin

Gavin didn't know what to expect as he climbed into the passenger seat of Aurora's 4Runner the following day after unhitching the flatbed from the vehicle.

"So you just drive around and . . .?" he asked, clicking the seat belt into place.

"Hop out and check the tanks. I have a long pole net in the back that I use to try and scoop any trash out of them."

She drove the vehicle out of the driveway and down the road. "We'll probably only be gone a few hours. I take a back road half the way through, and it makes for a nice loop."

"Why do I get the feelin' you enjoy this little escape?" Gavin rested his elbow on the joint armrest.

She turned left and headed east on State Route 287. "Because I do. It's my me time. Even if I spend it cleaning up other people's disregard for wildlife and nature. I love my girls, and they have school, so it's not like I have them 24-7, but I'm such an explorer, and sometimes it's nice to have time out of the house. I miss being able to take off in my plane or even go to the grocery store by myself."

"Thank you for letting me tag along durin' your alone time." Gavin watched as they passed the grocery store, the diner, and the post office. "I'm . . . leaving soon."

When he looked over at Aurora, she kept her focus on the highway, both hands on the steering wheel. "I figured it would be soon. You must want to assess the damage. I sure hope it's not too terrible."

He removed his cowboy hat and set it on his knee. "Unfortunately, I think it was a doozy, and I'm rather worried about what I'm goin' home to find."

"Sadly, from what I've seen on the news, I think you might be right." She turned off the highway and onto a dirt road.

The dust puffed up behind the 4Runner as the road stretched north. Short mountains with rounded peaks scattered across the horizon with taller jagged-topped mountains farther in the distance. He'd never seen so many shades of brown; it was almost like a painting brought to life from a talented artist who somehow made something that should be boring and plain rather delightful and mesmerizing.

"The first one is just off to the left here." Aurora pointed towards the passenger window. "Most of the snakes should be hiding with the cooler temps, but be careful all the same."

She put the 4Runner in park and hopped out. He joined her as they walked to a sun-bleached concrete square sticking out of the ground by about three feet. A few remnants of metal from a windmill were scattered around.

Aurora approached the edge and peered into it. He could see how if something jumped in here, it would never get out without help. The drop was straight down and at least ten feet deep.

"This seems like a long way out to use it for a trash can." He spotted a Circle K cup and candy wrappers, along with a broken tree branch and a few other random pieces of debris.

"People go off-roading out here, camping up and down the dry washes, and they're usually city folks. So I guess they think if they're far enough away, they don't have to respect the land since they're only visiting." She headed to the back end of her 4Runner and popped the hatch. "You know—out of sight, out of mind."

With the pool skimmer in hand, she scooped out the cup and wrappers and threw them in a trash bag she had folded up in the back. "Lots of mining around here back in the day, and there are a billion and one rusted-out cans and tin containers from the camps. Yet, the junk from today's people gets worse every year."

As they climbed back into the 4Runner, he sensed her frustration in the air. Aurora was passionate about the desert and it showed. Which only caused him to grow more attached and attracted to her. Everything he didn't need when he was already packing up his luggage.

She punched the radio, and classic country filtered through the speakers. "Is the music okay?"

"Yes, can't go wrong with the classics."

"It's a mixed CD, can't get any reception out here. Your cell phone won't have a signal either."

Gavin continued to watch the landscape ahead of them. "Bad place to break down."

"A long walk." She knocked on the dashboard with her fist. "Knock on plastic, so to speak."

Aurora drove farther down the dirt road, and greenery at the edge of a wash was visible out the passenger window. When she parked at the next stop, the sun was high and warm. As soon as he stepped out, a yip echoed in the nearby concrete pit.

Aurora approached the side wall and leaned over the raised ledge. "Crap."

He joined her and saw a young coyote inside, its eyes wide with fear and caution. "You think he's been down there long?"

"I have no idea. It hasn't rained in the valley in over a month, so he didn't jump in there for the water. He's thinner than he should be."

He readjusted his hat to block the sunshine. "Can you call the wildlife rescue?"

She shook her head as she jogged to the back end of the 4Runner. "They won't do anything." Aurora removed a thick tow rope with bold metal hooks at the end.

"And what are *you* plannin' to do with that?" His heartbeat sped up.

"Save it."

# Chapter 27

## Aurora

Aurora fed one end of the rope through the bull bar on the front of her 4Runner, looping it through, and yanking it tight. She'd done this once before with great success and hoped this would have the same outcome.

"Wait a minute." Gavin pointed forcefully. "You can't go in there?"

"Well, how else will the coyote get out?" She grabbed the rope with both hands and tugged it for good measure. Then dropping it at her feet, she headed towards the back of her vehicle once again.

Gavin followed her as she removed the pair of work gloves that were shoved into a side cubby. "I'll go down in there and get him." He reached for her gloves.

She squinted as she looked up at him; the sun was just over his hat. "And why is that?"

"Because—" His nose scrunched up like he smelled something terrible. "Just exactly what do you plan to do once you get down there?"

Aurora spun around, surveying the area. "I think I saw a pallet back there. We can use it as a ramp. Can you help me carry it?" She headed back in the direction they'd come from, Gavin hurrying by her side.

143

"How do you plan on gettin' the coyote to use a ramp?"

"I saw some branches over here too; I can corral it up and out. I've got food in the 4Runner to help in the transition. Let's hope this pallet works. I can get in and out with the rope, but the little guy will need the ramp."

She spotted the wood and hurried toward it. Aurora approached a sun-soaked pallet and poked it with her boot, moving it in the dirt enough to allow any hidden creatures, like a rattlesnake, to make themselves known.

Aurora put her left arm out, directing Gavin to back up. She used the tip of her boot to flip over the board. With nothing slithering out, she picked up one end, and Gavin grabbed the other. The six-foot board bowed like it was made of rubber as they hauled it closer.

"This is so flimsy. If we want it to hold together, I'm going to have to get myself in there first with the rope, I'll send the rope back up, and then you'll have to lower it down to me."

They approached the 4Runner, and she shifted the pallet into one hand and removed some dog food cans with pop-tops from a small bag she'd placed in there earlier.

"I don't like this idea," he mentioned as she shoved the cans into the waistband of her jeans like she was holstering a gun.

"I agree, it's not the best idea. But first, it's the only idea, and second, unfortunately, if we don't get the coyote out of there, he'll die." She helped him set the pallet against the lip of the concrete. "Since my back is going to be to him as I lower, I need you to keep an eye on him."

"No pressure," he winced. "In my past life, I was a coyote whisperer."

She patted his arm. "Great, I'm not worried."

"That makes one of us," he mumbled.

Aurora took a deep breath. She didn't want to scare the little guy, but she also needed to be careful. Her girls needed her, but so did this coyote.

She gripped the rope with both gloved hands and straddled the lip of the concrete box. Then, wrapping her hand around the rope to keep it from slipping, she pushed her left boot against the side of the wall, then her right boot, and repelled down the rope inch by inch, trying to look over her shoulder at the coyote. The stink of coyote urine filled her nose, and trapped heat radiated around her.

The animal was young, probably less than a year old. He didn't move towards her, choosing instead to hover behind a broken branch. She landed softly and released her hands from the rope, allowing Gavin to pull it back up. Tucking herself in the corner, she crouched down a bit to assess the situation. The pallet would work, but it wouldn't be easy. With the coyote hovering behind the mess of branches, he'd be reluctant to understand she was only trying to help him.

"Okay," she called softly up to Gavin. "Try your best to lower the board down."

The wood's edge blocked the sun for a second as Gavin lifted it and balanced it on the ledge above. She continued to check on the coyote out of the corner of her eye as the pallet was lowered. Thankfully, he was still hiding behind the debris.

As the board slid into her hands, she bent at the knees to allow it to gently come to rest on the ground. It would be a bit of a jump for the coyote to get up and over, but after the jump he'd taken into the tank, it would be nothing he couldn't handle.

She removed the canned food from her waist and tapped some of the food up the board.

"Grab those long sticks up there, off to the side," she called up.

He lowered them down as far as he could and then let go. Aurora stepped back as they dropped into the corner in front of her. She grabbed them and put one in each hand.

"Be careful," Gavin called down.

Aurora moved toward the coyote, who'd wedged himself into the opposite corner of the tank. She took the sticks and pointed them in a cone shape. As she approached the animal, he lunged and bit at the sticks.

"Sorry, buddy, but I need you to get up the ramp." She steadied the long sticks as he continued to bite at them.

As the coyote was near the ramp, Aurora paused, waiting to see if he'd take the bait. Accidentally, one of the sticks moved enough to tap the side of the pallet, startling the coyote. He scurried back into the corner she'd just worked hard at getting him out from.

"Dang it." She sighed and lowered the sticks.

Perspiration from the trapped heat caused her clothes to stick to her body, and her mouth grew dry. However, she wasn't about to give up, even when a sudden lightheaded feeling washed over her.

Observing the coyote from behind the shrub debris, he clearly had been down there for at least several days and needed to get out and find some food and water.

Aurora held one of the sticks up as she scooped a little bit of canned food onto it. Then, using both hands to control the stick, she eased it toward the coyote like a knight stick.

"Come on, buddy, it's food. I know you're hungry. It smells good, doesn't it?"

The coyote eyed the stick, then his nose moved, picking up on the scent.

"Good job, buddy. There's lots more." Aurora slowly inched the stick back and towards the ramp. And just like that, he followed the bait and stepped closer to the pallet, taking nibbles of the dog food along the way.

She coaxed him toward the ramp, where more of the food he was starving for literally sat. But it wasn't enough for the scared pup to trust, and noticing he was no longer in his hiding spot, he bolted to the opposite corner.

"It's okay. He knows the food is there. I'll get him out." Aurora stepped forward, the sticks pointed in front of her as sweat trickled down her forehead. It had to be over a hundred degrees in there. "Come on, little one. Freedom is just up the ramp."

With the sticks together like a cone, she guided him back around to the ramp and, this time, blocked him from going behind it.

"Stand back. If he runs for it and jumps, who knows where he'll land," Aurora called up.

"Be careful." Gavin's head allowed for a shadow to form above.

She directed the coyote to the board, and he spotted the food waiting for him. Aurora allowed him to take his time, eating up the first little bit at the base of it. Then, he stepped up, going for the next pile of wet dog chow. But when he took another step, the board shifted. The pup couldn't have weighed more than fifteen pounds, but the wood had been severely damaged by the sun that a dime might cause it to burst apart.

Aurora couldn't risk the board snapping because then the pup would be stuck for sure. She raised the sticks to either side of the board and took a loud step behind him at the base, hoping the noise would startle him into running the rest of the way up the ramp.

He finished the last of the food as she stomped again. That was all the coyote needed. He bolted up the ramp, making a grand leap over the edge to freedom. He cleared the top as Aurora let the sticks drop from her sore and weak hands. However, the sticks slammed onto the board, shattering it into pieces.

She leaned her head up to the sky. Now that the emergency was no longer, Aurora realized how much coyote pee was down there, the smell suddenly overpowering.

The rope hung loose into the tank, and she struggled to grip it due to her fatigue. Another wave of lightheadedness washed over her, and Gavin's shadow provided shade when she looked up.

"Are you planning on staying down there for a while?" he asked.

"Give me a minute." She didn't want to admit to her weakness, but she couldn't grip anything, let alone focus as her head spun with dizziness.

Shaking her hands out, she gripped the rope, but before she could attempt to climb up, it started to move.

"Hang on," Gavin said. "I'm pulling you up."

By the time she could refuse, Aurora was at the ledge, and Gavin had his arm out for stability while he continued to pull the rope taut. With the last of her energy, she flung her leg over, bending at the knee for added leverage, and then the rest of her body followed.

Stumbling forward, Aurora pushed her bottom into the side of the tank. When she placed her hands on her knees, Gavin's hand found her back. The fall breeze was welcome as it hit her sweat-covered clothes. His face was close enough she could see the grays peppered throughout his newly trimmed beard.

"I'm glad you're okay." His voice was reserved.

She nodded. "Me too, but I smell horrible."

"Don't worry about it. It's the scent of victory." He chuckled.

Aurora laughed a sigh, and when she stood up straight, pain coursed through her back. "Then I must smell like a silver medalist, at least. We should check on the other ones. It's later than planned, and the girls will be out of school soon."

Gavin stepped forward and enveloped his arms around her, pulling her close. "Definitely the scent of a gold medalist."

Aurora's arms slowly wrapped around him, returning the hug. As her legs wobbled, he held her upright, and if it wasn't for how horrible she smelled, it might not have ended at the hug.

She allowed her arms to fall from around Gavin, removed her gloves, and walked back to the 4Runner. Spinning around to open the driver's door, Aurora bit her lip. She might've had a nose full of coyote scent, but not enough that she couldn't smell Gavin's masculine cologne and still feel his arms around her.

# Chapter 28

## Gavin

As Aurora exited off the dirt road and back onto the high-way, Gavin spotted how small Woolsey appeared from outside town. The landscape was dotted with slips of life like a night sky of stars.

Thankfully, the other two stops had been quick to check the empty water basins with no more animals in need of rescuing.

"Do you have any tweezers?" He pushed his thumb against his middle finger.

She took her eyes off the road for a second and glanced at him. "Is everything okay?"

"It's a nasty splinter."

He saw her lips stretch at the sides. "I'm sorry. It must have been from the pallet."

When her right hand reached over, it landed softly on the underside of his wrist. He froze, holding his breath.

"Do you mind tagging along to get the girls with me, and then I can yank it out back at the house?" She smacked the steering wheel with her free hand. "Duh, we're driving right by Elizabeth's, so I'll just drop you off."

"My truck is back at your place. I'll go back with you."

"Right." She kept her hand on his wrist, and he hoped she couldn't feel his racing pulse. "Oh no, you're bleeding. That's not a *little* splinter."

"It's not a big deal, the bleedin'." He held the finger with the splitter out. The last thing he needed was to end up getting blood on anything, let alone shoving the wedge of wood further into his skin.

Aurora shook her head and brought the 4Runner to a complete stop at the sign where they turned to head to the city center and the school. She moved her hand from his wrist to the center console and pulled out a folded-up periwinkle-colored bandana. "Here, use this to soak up the blood. It's clean."

Taking the bandana, he carefully wrapped what he could of the wound. When he looked up, a woman wearing a long flowing purple-and-maroon dress waved from the corner.

Aurora rolled down her window. "Hey, Sydney! Glad to see you're back for the year."

Sydney approached the vehicle and placed her ring-covered fingers on the frame. "Hey-llo, Aurora, and why if it ain't, Gavin."

Aurora leaned back into the seat, and he could now see the post office's only employee.

"Hey, how are you doin'?" he asked, leaning forward in the seat.

"Good, and this weather, it's glorious. It's finally getting nice out. Gotta love fall, nothing like a nice stroll. There were no packages left for anyone to pick up, so I closed early."

"The weather is perfect. Hopefully, I can break out my sweaters soon." Aurora smiled.

"Don't we all hope for that," Sydney praised. "Off to get the girls from school?"

"Yes, we had a little rescue mission that needed our attention, and we're running a bit late."

"I won't keep you. See you around." Sydney gave a wave and crossed the street.

"I'm surprised y'all say things like that." Gavin leaned back in the seat as Aurora turned onto the street, and the school appeared through the windshield's view.

"Say things like what?"

"That you're happy summer is over. I figured you loved the heat and were sad to see it go."

"Just because we're good at handling the heat doesn't mean we enjoy it." She pulled into the circular driveway to Woolsey Elementary, joining a short line of cars already parked and waiting. A lone school bus sat at the head of the line.

Gavin squeezed the bandana tighter around his finger, grateful to see the bleeding had slowed. "Woolsey is laid back. It reminds me a lot of home. It's nice."

"I'm glad you enjoy it here." She turned in her seat and reached for his hand.

"I mean, look at *all* the hustle and bustle," he joked, motioning with his head at the calm scene in front of them.

"It's tough," she mocked, "but thankfully, the girls manage to make it to the car in one piece." She held his hand like it was a baby bird. "Are you sure your finger is okay?"

Aurora leaned closer to him, and even after a day of sweat and coyote urine, she still smelled of soft floral petals. *How is that possible?*

The bell for the school buzzed and teachers and students slowly filtered out. There must've been only a handful of them, making it easy to spot the girls.

Aurora hopped out as Ava yanked open the back passenger door and her mom got Willa's door.

When Ava climbed in, she spotted Gavin in the passenger seat. "Gavin! What are you doing here?"

As Willa buckled in, she said, "Gavin, hi," and gave a little wave.

He'd turned around in his seat and faced them, trying to hide his bloody finger. "I went to help your mom out today."

"Again?" Ava asked as she snapped in her seat belt.

"Are you tired of me already?" Gavin asked as Aurora returned to the driver's seat and grinned.

"No!" Willa laughed.

On the short drive back to Aurora's house, classic Brooks & Dunn played from the speakers, as Ava and Willa sang along. It had to have been their hundredth time listening to it because they knew every word. A twitch in his chest caused him to examine what was happening in that very moment. The familiarity of driving up to her house brought such a sense of serenity. His thoughts battled with the notion that he could keep this tranquility if things were different. Instead, he'd save the feeling and return to it when he missed the Easton girls.

"Go get washed up, girls, and put your backpacks away. I need to help Gavin."

They climbed from the 4Runner and made their way to the front porch. After unlocking the door, she kicked off her boots.

"Let me grab the tweezers, or maybe pliers." She took the steps one at a time behind the girls. "Take a seat at the island."

He remained standing by the front door, wanting to wait for her.

When Aurora bounded back down the steps, Gavin smiled. Yet, not any smile, but a geeky-falling-in-love smile like on prom night. And as soon as he realized he was doing it, he drew his lips into a straight line.

"The best light is in the kitchen," she paused, "you didn't need to wait for me. You're welcome to wander the house."

In the time she'd been upstairs, she changed from her jeans and pulled on a pair of baby-blue shorts, a worn and faded black tank top, and wrapped her hair into a loose ponytail.

Gavin took a seat at the barstool and rested his hand, palm side up on the island's cold surface. She washed her hands and then removed several supplies from a side drawer and slid onto the stool next to him. When Aurora took his hand in hers, tingles traveled up his arm as though he'd been electrocuted. As she drew her face closer, he felt her breath on his hand, and he remained as still as possible even though his heart pounded. He'd never been this close to her lips in bright lighting and noticed a freckle on the underside of her chin as she titled her head. Lost in a stare, the world stood still, and the tiny bit of irritating pain disappeared along with the time.

"Got it," her voice was soft. She held up the chunk of wood in the tweeters. "That was a big one. But it all came out clean, and I didn't need the pliers."

As he observed the chunk, he had no idea how she got it out without him even feeling a pinch. Aurora headed to the trash can, dropped the shard in it, and then moved to the sink to wash off the tweezers. She opened a nearby high cabinet and removed a box of Band-Aids. "I know most men aren't big on these but indulge me for a few hours to allow the alcohol to keep it cleaned out. It should be fine, but just in case."

When she handed the box of Band-Aids to him, their fingers brushed at the tips. Aurora stood there, frozen, their skin touching. He couldn't think of anything to say, he started to smile, and she mirrored him.

"Mom!"

Gavin took the box as Aurora stepped back and turned to Ava, entering the kitchen, holding a wrinkled piece of paper.

"Mom, you and Gavin have to finish the fall bucket list."

Aurora set her hand on Ava's head. "We finished the list, sweetie."

"No," Ava whined and shoved the paper near her mom's face.

Aurora took it from her daughter and examined it. He peered over the top of the paper and noticed some large handwriting with misspelled words. *Mom and Gavin go on a romentik dat.*

"See, Gavin can't leave yet." Ava pointed to the addition on the bucket list.

The corner of Aurora's lip turned up. "Hmm, I guess it does show we have one thing left, but sweetheart, Gavin is leaving soon."

"But if it's on the list, we have to follow it, right?" He winked at Ava. "I guess this means I'll have to stay an extra day."

Aurora shook her head. "No, you don't have to. I know you need to get home."

"It's on the list, and we must complete the list." He cocked a smile.

"Thank you," she mouthed as she handed Ava her list.

# Chapter 29

## Aurora

Aurora couldn't recall the last time she put on a dress—or, for that matter, anything fancy. The fabric felt snug against all the correct places, and as she swiped a coat of brown mascara over her lashes, her heart started to race. She wondered if it was possible to hear someone's heartbeat without leaning an ear against their chest.

She checked the time on her cell phone, two in the afternoon. The doorbell rang as she slid the wand back into the mascara tube.

"I got it!" Ava called out.

"Are you and Willa ready to go to Granny L's?" Aurora asked, stepping out into the hall at the top of the stairs.

"Pretty," Willa said, meeting her mom at the landing.

She held out her hand as she said, "Thank you." They descended the stairs together, and she felt as giddy as a teenager.

Ava held open the front door as Gavin stepped through wearing dark-wash jeans and a pale-blue striped dress shirt, rolled up at the sleeves.

When Aurora reached the final step, their eyes met.

"You look . . ." he fumbled.

"Pretty!" Willa cheered.

"Exactly," Gavin beamed.

He wasn't wearing his cowboy hat, and Aurora could spot a bit of curl in his brown hair. She clenched her hands together because she desperately wanted to reach out and run her hands through it.

"You look gorgeous!" Ava shouted.

"Thank you, honey. Are you girls ready for Granny L's?"

Ava lifted her backpack filled with coloring books, pens, and Barbies for her and Willa to play with while they were at Lillian's house.

"Okay, she's expecting you, so head on over." Aurora stepped next to Gavin, kissed her girls on their cheeks, and gave them a quick hug. "I'll see you both in time for bed tonight."

She stepped out onto the porch and watched as her girls skipped across the way, down the road, and onto Lillian's front yard.

Gavin held out his arm, and Aurora looped her hand through it.

"Are you ready?" he asked.

"Absolutely." She blushed.

Aurora had no clue what Gavin had planned for their date, but the butterflies in her stomach danced to a hectic beat. They'd been heading north on the I-17 for nearly two hours before exiting and entering a small town unfamiliar to Aurora. The road continued to weave and turn as they drove higher in elevation. Soon the green leaves were sprinkled with golds and yellows.

"When I looked up fall bucket list items online, I noticed it said to visit a winery," Gavin said, making another turn down a narrow winding road. "So, I figured that Ava's list was not one hundred percent accurate. But a child shouldn't be addin' a winery to their list, so I let it slide."

"We're going to a winery?" Aurora asked.

The butterflies in her stomach suddenly fluttered away. Were they going to the one that Mike had always said he'd take her to?

"I found this place. Lots of great views, and when I called, they said the leaves were at their peak."

She and Trinity had visited a few wineries since she lost her husband, but never the one that he'd promised. *Page Springs.*

"It's Page Springs. Have you been before?"

"I haven't." And with that, her stomach knotted up as though the butterflies were fighting each other.

He clicked on the turn signal, pulled the truck into the gravel drive off the main road, and parked it under a solar panel carport structure. To their right was a path going down a small, paved hill. Trees were plentiful around the winery, and the vines had all been harvested.

There was a small row of vines stretching up on a slope, and rolling hills of more vines in the distance at the end of the path. The winery used every square inch of its land to their advantage and labeled each section of grapes.

They climbed from the truck, and coming around the back end, nearly bumped into each other.

"I guess I need to be quicker at opening your door for you." He took hold of her arm, firm in his grasp, as though she might stumble otherwise.

She blushed. "I've always felt silly with stuff like that. I mean, I can open a door."

"I know you're capable of opening a door, but it's a nice thing to do." He stuck his elbow out, and she wrapped her hand around it. Their boots crunched over the gravel as they headed toward the main door, just past a small outside seating area under a canopy.

The main building was painted white with black trim and boasted a light wood-stained glass front door. Cool November air was enough to make one chilly but not cold. Gavin held the door open for Aurora as they entered.

Soft pine floors ran throughout and made a hollow noise under her boots as though they were walking on a second level. And they were, per the sign on the wall, since below was where they bottled the wine.

"Reservation for Gavin," he said to an employee in a Page Springs T-shirt.

"Right this way," she answered and pivoted on her heel.

They followed the hostess down a narrow hall, past the indoor tasting room, and out the door onto a compact patio with only five tables. The view overlooked the winery's rolling hills and scattered trees in muted greens, yellows, and ambers. Gavin pulled out a chair for Aurora as the hostess handed her a menu, and once he sat, she handed one to him.

"I'll let the waitress know you're here." She smiled and hurried back inside.

Aurora looked up from the menu and took in the view. The leaves rustled in the slight breeze, and a candle tucked into a tiny glass votive flickered between them on the waffled black tabletop.

"Is this the first time you've been to a winery?" Aurora asked.

"Believe it or not, this cowboy has been to a few. My friend owns a winery as well. Louisiana has many sweet wine blends, but they're better with specific dishes like cold kinds of pasta and cheese and crackers, unlike your basic reds and whites that can pretty much go with anythin.'"

"That sounds interesting. I don't believe I've ever had a sweet wine from the South." Her eyebrows arched. "I'd love to travel around and try wines from different states."

"If you're ever in Louisiana, I'll have to take you to one."

She returned her eyes to her menu. The comment hit her sinisterly in the heart. She was at the winery she'd always wanted to try with Mike yet was with another man. And it made her feel awkward and ashamed but also optimistic and enchanted. There was no denying they'd remain friends, and of course, she'd visit Louisiana, yet the conflicts raging in her mind were enough to cause her anxiety to rise.

"Is everythin' okay?" Gavin leaned over his menu just as the waitress returned.

"Can I get you started on a nice red or white, or maybe you'd like to try a flight?"

"A flight would be great." Gavin glanced at the menu. "I'll have the combo flight."

"That sounds great. I'll do that too," Aurora added.

"Do you want me to put in an order for food or are you still deciding?" she asked.

"I'm goin' with the meat pizza," Gavin said.

"Make it two pizzas, but I'll do Margherita." Aurora handed her menu up to the waitress.

"Perfect, I'll be right back." She snatched the menus before turning to a nearby table.

He folded his hands together in front of him, his Band-Aid still intact. "Are you okay?"

Honestly, she had no idea how to answer his question. Telling the truth would be everything and nothing at the same time. How could she tell him she's falling for him *and* feels entirely disloyal to her late husband? Instantly, her bottom lip quivered.

The deck below her chair appeared to spin, and she placed both hands flat on the table.

"Aurora, are you feelin' alright? We can go if you want—just say the word."

She shut her eyes and shook her head. Then, keeping her eyes closed, she could hear the faint sound of water running, a river gliding over rocks. The scent of bark and foliage danced against her nose. When Aurora opened her eyes, she stared down at the tabletop. "Mike and I were supposed to come here."

When she raised her head, Gavin's skin was pale. His eyes locked on hers, and he shifted to stand up, the chair sliding on the wood planks below. "Let's go."

Aurora stuck out her hand, waving it. "No, no." She motioned for him to sit back down.

He eased into the chair as though it might break under his weight. "I'm so sorry. I should've thought better."

"How could you've known?"

The waitress appeared with two tumbler-style stem-less glasses and a welcoming smile. But once she started to pour the flight and describe it, Aurora had zoned out, staring at the pear-colored liquid splashing into the glass. Mike was never coming back. He could never bring her here, no matter how much she wished for it. No matter how long she kept waiting. She couldn't continue avoiding things.

But the wind brought the question of why. Why should she feel negative about this experience? It was not something she and Mike shared. There was no memory of him behind a corner or around a vine. If she gave up everything they'd planned to do, she'd never leave the darn house.

Aurora raised her glass toward Gavin and forced a smile across her lips. "To new experiences with great company."

Gavin's mouth twitched up, just as unsure as she was. And without a word in response, they tapped glasses.

# Chapter 30

## Gavin

Gavin felt terrible about enjoying their dinner together as much as he had. The outside temperature was comfortable, the pizza was tasty, and the wine was crisp. Of course, the view of both nature and Aurora were perfect. But he'd messed up and should've thought better about picking a winery without at least checking with Trinity to make sure it wouldn't trigger memories for Aurora.

They simultaneously eased back in their chairs, leaving the remaining slice of pizza, one each, on their plates.

"Can I get you a to-go box?" the waitress asked, approaching the table.

"Yes, and I'd like to purchase a couple of bottles of wine also. Aurora, did you have one you liked?"

Her mouth fell open. "Oh gosh, you don't have to." She waved her hand at the notion.

Gavin squeezed his eyes in a disconcerting fashion. "I want to." He gave a side glance up at the waitress.

Aurora pressed her lips together before breaking out into a smile. "The grenache was fabulous."

"Wonderful selection. And for you." The server turned to Gavin.

"I'll take the Syrah."

"I'll be right back."

"Thank you," Aurora set her napkin on the table, shoving it under the thin tin pizza plate. "You didn't have to. I can pay for it."

"There is one thing you should know." Gavin cleared his throat. "You can get away with opening your own doors, but when it comes to meals and special treats, I pay."

She held her hands up. "Okay, cowboy." Aurora flashed a quick smile, and he swore his heart stopped long enough for him to lose his breath.

Once their leftovers were packed up, the wine bagged, and the bill paid, Gavin held his arm for Aurora to loop her hand through. As they returned to the parking lot, Gavin stated, "Wait here, I'll go stick this in the car."

She remained in her spot as Gavin trotted to the truck. There was a man pacing back and forth off to the left of the building, talking in a hushed tone on his phone. And when Gavin returned to Aurora's side, she pointed at the stranger with her eyes.

"Mike used to do that," she whispered as she drew close to Gavin's side.

Craving to wrap his arm around her waist and pull her even closer caused his fists to clench with desire.

"He'd always be on the phone trying to get to the bottom of an issue, and honestly, I don't miss that part. He was always about work, work, work. Mike's work ethic provided us with the riches we have, but it was at a cost. And I've vowed never to allow my nonprofit to take over my life."

Gavin continued to watch the man on the phone as she spoke. When he made eye contact with Aurora, her face appeared solemn, lost between relief and sadness.

"Would you like to go on a little adventure?" His elbow outstretched. "Away from anyone on their phone?"

Aurora took hold of his bicep, her palm gentle against his muscle. "Of course."

He followed the instructions the hostess had given him, unbeknownst to Aurora, and guided her down the steep slope leading to the vineyard's base. Following the path to the right, they passed a small rough-wooded cottage and then to a vine-wrapped trail. They went farther down the hill and soon found themselves at a small picket gate.

Gavin pushed the flimsy weathered wood, causing it to swing open. At first, he was going to allow Aurora to enter ahead of him. However, noticing the path was rocky and slippery, he moved his hand behind his back for Aurora to take hold of.

Leading the way down, she wrapped her fingers around his palm, and with each step forward, the sound of rushing water grew louder. And just as the trail leveled, the river appeared to the right of the trees. Velvet ash, cottonwoods, and Arizona walnut trees on both sides of the stream filtered the sunshine.

"Let's get closer," she suggested with a childlike enthusiasm in her voice.

Gavin widened his stance and held out his hand. The flat boulders held little pools of water and were slippery underfoot. Pockets of river water flowed into crevices near the edge and fallen gold leaves floated in the stagnant water.

Standing side by side on the rock, Aurora hadn't let go of his hand since the top of the hill at the gate. The temperature had dropped by a few degrees by the water, and a chill coursed through him. It was a little heavenly oasis break from the cactus and dry dirt of Woolsey. A canary yellow butterfly drifted into view, and they watched it decide where to land for a rest.

"I hope you don't think back on our time here and feel that this was disrespectful to Mike." Gavin gazed down at her, their height difference glaringly obvious with them side by side.

Aurora squeezed Gavin's hand as she looked up at him; the wind caused her hair to flutter. "Absolutely not, it's so . . . peaceful down here. Thank you for bringing me and sharing this with me."

He faced her, reached his hand out, and tucked some hair behind her left ear. Allowing his thumb to linger on her cheek, Gavin leaned down, drawing his lips near Aurora.

From his toes to his head, every muscle in his body wanted him to kiss her. But just as he was about to lean further in, the flash of Mike's face, one he saw in a picture frame back at Aurora's house, caused him to nearly jump backward. No matter how much he wanted it, and his heart craved it, he couldn't. Gavin had to allow Aurora to make the first move—if there was one to make or the time to make it.

A sigh escaped her mouth, and Aurora glanced around Gavin as his hand slid from her cheek to her waist. He followed her gaze, spotting a couple on the deck above, at the edge of the ledge of rocks. They gave a wave to Gavin and her.

She turned back toward the river and whispered, "I hope they don't think I was staring at them. They caught me off guard. I wasn't aware there was a deck there, and I couldn't see it with the trees. They appeared like ghosts hovering above."

Gavin laughed. "We'll have to go and see what else is up there."

"I wish we could stay here for a while longer, but I told the girls I'd be home in time to tuck them in."

"It is peaceful. Maybe you can come back with the girls. I'm sure they'd love to see the river, maybe try to skip some rocks over there"—he pointed over her shoulder—"where it slows."

"A wonderful idea." Aurora stepped and paused to glance back at him when her right boot slipped on the rock. Her arms waved frantically as she began to fall backward. He lunged, thrusting his hands forward, and caught her under the arms before her bottom hit the rocks.

"That was close," they said in unison.

She relaxed in his arms and leaned her head back, looking straight up at Gavin, and produced a smile of relief. "I'm glad I'll be leaving here without a broken butt."

"I'm grateful to have prevented a broken bottom." Gavin raised his arms, hoisting her back to standing.

"Thank you." She fixed her hair, pushing it back behind her ears. "That would've been a long, wet, uncomfortable drive home."

"Don't get too ahead of yourself. We still have to get to the top, and you already used your butt insurance coverage."

"That was only my out-of-the-*back* pocket deductible I used."

Gavin smirked and held his hand out. "For safety—insurance protocol."

She took his hand in hers as he stepped in front of her. His hand went behind his back so she could hold on to it as they made their way back up the hill to the gate.

"Let's go see if we can find that deck before we leave." Even though the ground was level and dry, Gavin continued to hold Aurora's hand.

Side by side, they wove around the Arizona Sycamores and came upon a vertically placed deck at the edge of the ledge. Making their way to the railing, their hands finally parted and rested upon the worn wood.

"The view is spectacular." She leaned forward, and he noticed her boots came off the deck.

They could see the river stretching from around the bend, the shades of golden leaves, like a Bob Ross painting, scattered the land below. Minutes passed as they remained lost in the view, and his hand found her back. Wishing he could stop the pull to be closer to her, the feeling nearly overwhelmed him.

She turned in his direction. "Thank you again. This was the most delightful afternoon."

Without her hand in his, he shoved his fist into his front jean pockets as they returned to the path, walking under the vines running overhead on a trellis leading back up to the main building when Gavin paused.

"Is everything okay?" she asked.

He nodded and looked back from where they came, the river was no longer in view, but the memory of today would be etched in his mind forever. And when he turned back around to face Aurora, she'd stepped closer to him than expected—caught off guard, his hands cupped her waist. His eyes rested on her mouth and then back to her eyes.

Gavin felt her hand on his hip and the other on his back. He moved his right hand and set it on her chin, and she blushed instantly. She closed her eyes and pushed her head against his hand. Then, Aurora pulled back, far enough for his hand to fall as she rested her cheek against his chest. Hoping she couldn't hear his heartbeat racing, or at least not connect the dots that she was causing it, he wrapped his arms around her. Her arms found their way around him, and without a word between them, he knew she was crying.

# Chapter 31

## Aurora

Aurora wiped her tears and did a quick check in the vanity mirror of Gavin's truck while he was inside the winery using the restroom. Rubbing her smeared mascara off the bottom of her lower lashes, Aurora pressed her lips together. She didn't know what had come over her at that moment with Gavin—why she'd cried so suddenly. So she chalked it up to having to do with something new or at least the area's beauty.

She flipped the vanity mirror back in place, and a couple walking out of the winery's front door caught her attention. The man carried a baby's car seat in one hand and wrapped his other around the woman's shoulder.

The same emotion that came out of nowhere rose inside of Aurora, again. Of course, she never forgot about it, and she never would. But she'd been good for so long at hiding the memory, pushing it deep inside her. The biggest secret of her life; she hadn't even shared it with Trinity.

Watching the couple with the baby draw closer to the truck, Gavin emerged in the distance from behind the winery's door. His wide stride was apparent in his walk, the way his strong shoulders seemed to hold his posture even taller than his six-foot frame. As the thoughts of a few moments ago held tight, Aurora pinched her eyes tightly closed, trying to rid them of moisture just as the driver's side door popped open.

"Alright," he said, sliding into this seat, "you ready to head home?"

She bit her lip as the sensitivity attached to the secret caused her chin to quiver. "Mm-hmm, yeppers."

As Gavin turned the classic country music on low, the truck made its way back onto the main road, and Aurora rested into the seat and shut her eyes. Unaware if she drifted to sleep or into meditation, when she opened her eyes, the sun had lowered enough on the passenger window that it caused her to squint.

"I know I said we needed to get back, but do you mind if we make a quick stop? With the rain the other night, I think it'll be great."

Gavin glanced over at her and then back out the windshield. "Sure, of course."

"Is everything okay? We don't have to."

He shook his head. "No, sorry." Moving his right hand to his lap and then back to the wheel, he said, "I was thinking about my house, back home. There was a television on inside the winery when I exited the bathroom."

She turned to him, instinctively reaching out to set her hand on his bicep. "Is it bad?"

Keeping his eyes on the road, it curved around a bend as a sports car revved past. "The national news reported that Crowley Parish, which has a bigger population than my county, not to mention better resources, is looking to be without power for another ten days, and some still don't have the water turned back on yet."

Aurora rubbed her hand back on and forth on his shirt. "Oh, that's horrible."

"The governor mentioned to those of us who left not to come back yet." Gavin punched the off button on the music as though upset by the song. "I understand the governor's request, but if it's that bad, I need to be there to help my neighbors. Small communities are the ones with the most to lose because they can't afford to leave."

"The news always portrays those who stay behind as foolish."

"It's definitely not a safe idea, but what the news forgets to mention is the cost of leaving. Getting a hotel if you don't have a family to stay with or the simple task of putting gas in your car for the drive, meals out . . . it adds up."

Aurora faced the front and brought her hands together in her lap. "I'm glad you were able to come out here and at least be safe, even if your home was not. Is there anything I can do to help?"

"Just keep being you." He glanced over at her but didn't smile like he usually did.

She didn't know what he meant by that, but now was not the time to ask. So, with the solitude of their thoughts, they spent the next thirty minutes listening to the road under the tires.

"If you're still up for making that stop"—Aurora pointed at the road sign for the next exit, one mile ahead—"you'll want to take this upcoming exit."

"I am. I'm curious to see what we're stoppin' for, although I hope not food because I'm still full from the pizza. Surprising, because it wasn't that big."

Butterflies swarmed in her stomach as Gavin turned off the highway. "Take a right here."

He flipped his signal on and followed her directions down several town roads and up a short hill coming to the opening of a park.

"You can park anywhere." She undid her seat belt even though they were still moving. "With the rain the other night and it being dusk, we should have a great show."

Pulling the truck into a spot, he shut off the engine. "Are we the only ones here?"

Aurora popped open the passenger door. "Seems that way."

By the time Gavin's boots hit the pavement, she was at his side and had grabbed his hand. "You're sure excited."

Like one of her daughters, she pulled him forward and to the edge of the neglected grass. The park looked the same as it had every other visit, and she wove around the thick mass of juniper trees and desert willows. Picnic tables were scattered under the canopy of a few as Aurora picked up her speed.

"The sun is nearly setting, and I don't want to miss it." She continued to hold his hand, directing him to follow by her side.

Coming to a path with flowering yellow bells and bright orange honeysuckle, she knew they made it just in time. Halting, she stopped at the start of the trail and let go of Gavin's hand.

"Wow." Gavin moved his hands to his hips. "It's . . ."

"The best botanical garden that no one talks about. I love coming here but haven't been since before Ava was born."

All around were brightly colored hummingbirds and butterflies in different shades of yellow.

"It's dinnertime for them. Just as the sun starts to disappear on the horizon, the recent rain on the flowers causes them to come out."

Reaching her hand toward Gavin, he took it, and they walked forward on the path, allowing the butterflies and hummingbirds to flutter past them. She paused in her steps and remained in place, surrounded by the sweet aroma of honeysuckle. There were so many wings surrounding them, the hum filled the air, invoking a sound almost robotic in its sheer volume.

Gavin squeezed her hand, and when she looked over at him, he was already staring at her. When their eyes met, Aurora faced him, unsure if it was the beauty around them, his charisma and charm, or simply wanting to escape her reality of loss. But he stood there, gazing down upon her, nature encircling them. His hands wrapped around her hips, then one quickly slid up to her chin, and she saw his vision go from her eyes to her lips.

The height difference between them became obvious as he moved his hands yet again, wrapping them around her waist in a hug and pulling her feet off the ground, bringing her lips closer to his.

They both froze, analyzing each other's mouths. Aurora's heartbeat was so loud it drowned out the wings of the butterflies and the *chirp-clicks* of the hummingbirds. With her hands wrapped around his neck, she was grateful he'd left his cowboy hat in the truck as she moved her fingers through his soft-as-velvet hair.

Aurora took a breath, he pulled her head toward his, and then he pushed his lips to hers. It was as though she'd possessed the desire to kiss Gavin in her heart for too long that allowing it to happen caused an explosion of passion. She couldn't physically get any closer to him, yet she continued to squeeze her arms around him as though doing so would melt them into one.

When they parted, Gavin lowered her back to the ground but kept his arms wrapped around her. All Aurora could think about was how she hadn't felt her heart beat so fast since that last spin class she went to in Cactus City. Bringing her hand to her heart, she allowed it to vibrate under her palm as though doing so meant she wasn't dreaming.

"Was that alright?" Gavin's hand was still firm on her back. "I didn't want to pressure you. It's . . ." He took a step backward, and his hands fell to his sides. "I've wanted to kiss you since the grocery store." He ran both hands through his hair. His face was flustered. "I'm sorry I couldn't take it anymore. I had to, and I'm sorry if that was wrong of me."

Aurora grabbed the front of his button-down shirt and pulled him forward, toward her lips, and kissed him again. Only this time, she knew she was doing it to try and keep the tears from falling. To keep the yelling inside her mind hushed. She didn't understand why she'd wanted to come here, now, with Gavin, but when they parted from their kiss, Aurora realized she'd done it to tell him the secret, to finally set it free. And although Aurora didn't know why she felt secure in telling him, she knew she needed to allow it to escape, to find a way to move on. She had to confide her secret to Gavin because it was eating her heart in two.

"I found out I was pregnant and was trying to figure out a special way to tell Mike we were going to have another baby. But he'd been working extra because of the changes within the company. They'd eliminated half of the sales team, and he'd started having to travel farther than ever before. The morning he was supposed to fly home, he had an aneurysm and never even got on the damn plane."

"I'm . . . oh, Aurora, I'm sorry."

Before she knew what was happening, Gavin had wrapped her into his arms, and she started to cry with such distress that her legs grew weak. He scooped her up, and when the sobbing stopped and she eased open her swollen eyes, she was sitting on the top of a picnic table overlooking the small pond, under a desert willow.

Aurora wiped what remained of her mascara from under her eyes with her pointer finger. "I held that secret in for so long."

Gavin stood in front of her, his hand on her shoulder. "No one knew?"

"No one." Aurora reached for his hand and weaved it around hers. "I didn't want to tell anyone because I didn't want anyone to have an added reason to feel sorry for me. But you know small towns."

His other hand moved from her shoulder to her hair, and he brushed it with his fingers as chills traveled down her back from his touch. "Do you mind me asking what happened to the baby?"

Aurora wiggled her upper body, sitting up straight. "I lost the baby. I had a miscarriage a few weeks after Mike's death. Thankfully, the girls were at a sleepover with Jolie, and I was able to speak with my doctor privately. Other than some pain and a few hours in the ER, I was able to go home and rest without anyone in town finding out."

"What a horrible thing to go through alone." Gavin's hand found her cheek, and she pressed her hand on top of it and closed her eyes.

"Well," she laughed a snarky huff. "This day is wrapping up super depressing."

"Do you think you'll have more kids?"

Aurora pushed herself up and off the top of the picnic table. "I haven't given it any thought. My body and mind have been trapped in memories of what could've been for so long that I stopped living for myself. I've been living only for my girls."

What she didn't add was that she hadn't given any thought to it until she realized falling in love again was possible. And that's precisely what scared her more than anything in the current moment. She couldn't stop herself from falling in love with Gavin.

# Chapter 32

## Gavin

Gavin knew Aurora wasn't ready for a relationship and didn't want to push her, no matter how much he enjoyed the spark when they kissed. He needed to go home before his feeling grew even more. His bags were packed, and his life awaited him back in Louisiana, so why did he feel like he had heartburn? Gavin's chest tightened as he pulled into Aurora's driveway and parked his truck.

By the time he climbed out, Aurora and her girls were already walking towards him. Ava had a bag in her hand that seemed to weigh as much as she did, for she struggled holding it off the ground. He hurried over to her, kneeling to her level.

"This is for you, Gavin." Ava attempted to hoist it up higher.

He took the paper bag with an orange and brown bow tied around the handle. "Thank you."

Gavin remained squatting, resting his elbows on his knees. "I had so much fun completin' the fall bucket list with you. And spendin' suppers with y'all was great too."

"Do you have to go?" Willa placed her hand on his shoulder like an adult might.

"The girls wanted to make sure you had stuff for your drive back home." Aurora stepped closer to Ava, who was making letters in the dirt with her shoe. "They're having a hard time with you leaving."

Gavin sighed. "I didn't mean for that to happen."

"I know."

"Ava, thank you." He motioned to the bag. "Be sure you have your mom check the mail because I'm going to be sendin' you somethin' great once I get back." He hoped the gesture would make the girls focus on something in the future and ease the separation.

"Okay," Ava mumbled and went to her mom's side.

"Thank you so much for stopping by to say goodbye," Aurora said. "Girls, remember Gavin is always welcome to come back."

"I promise I'll see y'all soon."

"He has helped us out a lot, and we had so much fun," Aurora added.

"Nothing lasts forever," Ava said. "That's what Mrs. Melissa told us in class when the plant died."

"Ava." Gavin knelt again. She walked back over to him. "Do you think you can do me a favor?" She nodded and pressed her hands together. "I need you to make us a bucket list for Christmas. Do you think you can do that?"

Ava smiled and nodded. "Yes, I can. I'm going to start it now." She gave Gavin a quick hug and hurried toward the house.

"Do you want to give Gavin a hug before he goes?" Aurora asked Willa, stroking her hair.

Willa nodded her head, and he kneeled to hug the little girl.

"I'll be back soon, okay, Willa?" Gavin said.

She returned to her mom's legs.

"Thank you so much for all you did to help with the wind-mills. I doubt I'll find better assistance when I do the rest around the state. We had a blast doing so many things with you. We'll miss you for many reasons."

"I wish I could stay longer, but . . ." Everything around Aurora and Willa faded into a filtered blur.

"You have to go home. And if anyone understands how important home is, it's me." She raised a hand back at the house. "History keeps us all rooted."

Gavin half-smiled. "I've never felt so at home and yet been so far from it. Thank you for allowing me to spend time with you and the girls. It was somethin' I never expected."

"You'd better get going," Aurora said, biting her lower lip, "you've got a long drive ahead."

"Do you know what my favorite thing about you is?" Aurora shook her head and glanced down at her daughter. "When your heart is hurting, you bite your lip." He stepped forward.

She wrapped her arms around him as Willa remained strapped to her mom's leg. Gavin breathed in Aurora's scent, hoping to keep it in his nose long after he left. When they parted, the urge to kiss her was nearly overwhelming. But with Willa there, it didn't feel appropriate. Aurora was just far enough away from him to be able to gaze up. Gavin couldn't stop staring at her lips. They were so close to his; all he had to do was pull her closer to him.

"Willa, could you please go inside and get your sister," Aurora said without moving back from him or looking away.

Gavin took his eyes off her for a second and saw Willa hurry toward the house and march up the steps just over Aurora's shoulder. When he went to refocus on her, he felt their lips meet. He might be a strong man, but he swore his knees quivered at that moment. Her lips tasted like coconut mint, and when she pulled her mouth off his, Gavin leaned in as though to chase her. She allowed it, and he lost track of time until they parted for good.

"My favorite thing about you is how safe you make me feel," she whispered and set her hand on his chest. "I'll miss you."

"You have no idea," he whispered.

The girls appeared on the porch, and Gavin stepped back. He'd known why she had Willa go inside; it was far too complicated to explain the kiss to them. Hanging out, having suppers, and going on adventures together was one thing, but a man—not their father—kissing their mom would cause an unneeded stir in their life.

"Don't forget," he pointed at them, "I'll be back for Christmas, so have that list ready."

Gavin continued to walk back to his truck, and when he reached it, he gave a final wave. He paused, gripping the keys before popping the door and finally shoving them into the ignition, bringing the engine to life with a twist of the wrist. As he drove off to the main road, he couldn't stop looking in his rearview mirror at the trio standing there waving beyond the dust his truck kicked up.

He wrung the steering wheel when he stopped at the sign before turning east onto State Route 287. Approaching the four-way stop, he took in the town one last time, and tapping the gas, he inched through without seeing another vehicle in sight.

The parking lot was packed at the diner, and a few cars were scattered at the grocery store, and one at the hardware store. As he eased past the post office, a car was pulling out, and he gave a wave but was unsure who the driver was that waved back. Woolsey was not much different than Jesser Parish; a wave was for everyone.

Gavin continued down the highway, finding a local country station on the radio, and turned the volume up. Of all songs, it was the same one he'd heard when he and the girls were heading up north for the first time to go on the fall bucket list hike. He cranked it up louder, hoping the noise would drown out the sadness encasing his heart.

No matter what, Gavin needed to go home. His entire life was there, even if some of it had been swept away by the storm, he could rebuild. Aurora and her kids weren't going to uproot their lives, and he couldn't uproot his. But as he clocked mile after mile away from Woolsey, he didn't know why he felt so melancholy. Sighing, he pushed himself snuggly into the seat and gazed at the endless road ahead of him.

# Chapter 33

## Aurora

Aurora set the bottle of Vino del Barrio Blanca from Page Springs on the coffee table after pouring a glass for herself and Trinity.

"How's the planning for Thanksgiving going?" Aurora asked and took a sip of the crisp white wine.

"My mom is insistent, as always, on doing it all herself. I told her that I can at least help with the side dishes."

"I offered to help Lillian, too. She waved me off. It's far too much work for one person to handle. But at least she's agreed to let me host it in the hanger. With the plane gone, we can easily fit the tables we need in there for everyone."

Trinity pushed her long hair over her shoulder and swirled the wine in her glass. The girls were spending the day with their Uncle Camden, and without a doubt, they were having fun with the dogs and maybe even the Hackenburgs were over with their kids.

"Can you believe how time flies, especially during the fall? Once October hits, it's nothing but a blur." Aurora picked at the tassels on a fuzzy blue blanket draped over the back of the couch.

"This wine is delicious, and yes, I agree—so fast. Too fast. I swear Jolie is growing out of her shoes weekly. Every time I put a shirt on her, it's like the hot water in the washer shrank it. But we know this time of year is the only time the water comes out cold."

"I don't miss the girls' terrible twos or the insane amount of clothing they went through." Aurora took another sip. "Gavin and I had such a lovely time at Page Springs. It was peaceful. I was not prepared for how hard it would be on the girls when he left."

"And hard on you, too."

"Maybe."

"Have you talked to him since he left?"

Aurora took a sip of wine. "We've texted a bunch and talked on the phone a few times. He only got back to Jesser a day ago and sounded overwhelmed with the amount of cleanup work that needed to occur. We've mostly spoken at night after the girls have gone to bed."

"And the girls?"

"They miss him, and Ava will try to stay up so she can talk to him. I couldn't believe how quickly he fit into our lives and then how quickly he was gone. I feel like maybe I messed up by allowing him in." Aurora signed. "And the kiss."

"The kiss," Trinity echoed, "is nothing you should feel guilty about. Mike wouldn't want you to carry on acting like you're married."

"How am I supposed to know what's right and what's wrong? I've read all the moving-past-the-death-of-a-spouse books, and they all say it's different for everyone, the grieving and finding new love." She rubbed her forehead. "I don't know how to feel, but I know that I was falling in love with Gavin, and him not being here hasn't made my feelings dissipate."

"But he doesn't live here. So what can you do?"

Aurora set her wineglass on the coffee table and snatched the blanket, gripping it between her fingers. "I need to figure out what I want, what's best for the girls and me."

Trinity leaned forward on the couch. "What does that mean?"

"I need to find out if he feels the same way and what we do about it."

"You mean to tell me you two haven't discussed the kiss or anything relationship-wise?" Trinity glanced around as though the answer was on the walls.

Aurora used her pointer finger and thumb to pinch her bottom lip together. "No. I mean, we were both there. So, what's there to discuss?"

"A kiss is never just a kiss."

"It can be." Aurora folded her arms over the blanket.

"Yeah, if you're stubborn, like my mother." Trinity threatened to toss a pillow in Aurora's direction. "What if Gavin wants you to move to Louisiana? Can you give up Woolsey? Can you give up your family home?"

Aurora clenched her teeth. "I don't know. There are so many great memories here, with the community, this house; it's all the girls know. It's all I know. Yet maybe those memories are a little suffocating. Everything, everywhere I look . . . I see Mike. I see us."

Aurora stood with her wineglass and walked to the French doors overlooking the backyard, taking in the view she'd known for all her life. "But there is no us anymore. I feel like I'm half, half of something missing. And it's the worst feeling right now. I'm exhausted from the weight of it. When Gavin was here, it started to fade, and the girls were happy, like before . . . before . . ." Tears filled her eyes instantly, and when she took a sip of wine, the liquid lodged in her throat, like the

184

misery prevented her from being able to swallow. When she finally did, it hurt as though she'd swilled down shards of glass.

"Do you think if Gavin felt the same way about you that he would move to Woolsey?"

Aurora shook her head and glanced down at her bare feet. She wiped her tears as she returned to the couch. "I don't want to ask him to leave his life behind. I can't ask him that."

"Why not?"

"Because we aren't in a relationship. That's something you ask if you're a couple. Plus, he might feel like living here would be replacing Mike, not starting fresh."

"Because you asked him?" Trinity's eyes rose.

"How can I ask him something like that? It's assuming he feels the same way about me as I do him."

"He kissed you. I might not have spent as much time with Gavin as you have, but he is honest and doesn't waste time spreading fluff. He kissed you because he wanted to. And I'd guess he wanted to long before you wanted him to."

Aurora was not about to tell her best friend she was right. Trinity already knew by the way she sipped her wine without taking her eyes off her. "Okay, how about you go to Louisiana and talk to him in person?"

"I can't go to Louisiana, I have the girls, and they have school. I don't want to complicate it more for them. Besides, he said he'd be back out at Christmas time. The last thing he or that town needs, is a visitor when they're trying to get their lives back up and running. There wouldn't even be a place to stay."

"Waiting never did anyone any good." Trinity swirled the wine in her glass. "You'll need to babysit Jolie so Camden and I can go to Page Springs. This wine is wonderful."

"Deal, as long as you bring back some La Serrana for Thanksgiving."

"Have you asked the girls what they want?" Trinity asked.

"They shouldn't have any wine."

Trinity shook her head and laughed.

Aurora sank deep into the couch as she exhaled. "I'm not dragging the girls into anything more with Gavin. It'll only cause more issues than it already has done."

"Exactly, my point. Asking them will help them feel included, and their answer is important. Has Elizabeth spoken to you yet?"

"I've been avoiding her, which has taken a great deal of energy. I had to hide in the grocery store behind the cereals, which led Charlie to ask what I needed, and that's how I ended up with eight boxes of Fruit Rings. And of all the sugary cereals, it's the only one the girls don't like." She rolled her eyes.

"Serves you right, speak with Elizabeth. Maybe she knows something you don't."

"You might be right. I mean, she talks to Gavin pretty regularly." Aurora rested her hand on the back of the couch. "So, Thanksgiving . . ."

"Don't change the subject." Trinity crossed her legs. "So, when do you leave for Louisiana?"

Aurora scrunched up her face. "What if he doesn't want me there? What if I have my feelings and his feelings all wrong?"

"That's why you *must* go. Talk to him in person, figure it out. And figure out if there is a relationship to discover. As long as *you're* ready."

"I hope I'm not letting everything slip through my fingers." Aurora took a long, lingering sip of wine, allowing it to coat her throat. "I don't want to make a mistake."

"It's only a mistake if you know the answer and allow your dreams to slip away."

Aurora only knew what her heart felt, and lately, it'd been aching for Gavin.

# Chapter 34

## Gavin

Gavin had spent the better part of the last two days moving the broken tree limbs scattered around his property into a nice pile as close to the main road as possible. He'd have Mark's Tree Removal come and haul it away once they could find a spot on their very booked calendar.

He shut off the backhoe's engine, removed his soiled work gloves, and proceeded to make fists and release them. After Arizona, it took a few days to get used to the humidity seeping back into his bones. He chuckled at the thought, something he honestly never would've noticed had he not stayed so long in the dry desert.

Jumping down from the machine, Gavin turned back around to view his home and was reminded of how much more work he had to do before it would be back to normal—not just the exterior. Inside, the water had receded but left the hardwood floors, half of the drywall, and baseboards damaged. Everything would need to be ripped out and replaced at a high cost. Unfortunately, every year the price of lumber went up, and at this point, Gavin didn't have a clue how much it would hurt his bank account. The insurance company would only cover the basic costs, not the high-quality materials he'd used.

"Maybe it's time to switch to tile." But he knew even at that, it could be damaged if it sat under water for too long. "Perhaps it's time to rebuild the house on stilts."

Gavin's land was inland far enough, and he shouldn't need to do such a build. Yet, this most recent hurricane proved otherwise. He adjusted his cowboy hat and noticed more missing shingles on his roof.

"Gavin!"

He glanced over his shoulder in the direction of his name being hollered.

"Gavin, you're back!"

His neighbor from across the street, Jeanna Ray, came down his overgrown grass and debris-filled drive. Her rust-colored hair was as wild as a hurricane, and her outfits were always a T-shirt and jean overalls. Gavin couldn't remember the last time he'd seen her with shoes on her feet, and even now, with all the glass and whatnot laying around, she hadn't changed out of her flip-flops.

"Jeanna Ray, hello. How are you doin'?"

She stopped and let a loud sigh slide from her mouth. "Just a real fine mess we all got ourselves in here now, ain't it?"

"I believe the worst one we've had yet." Gavin tipped his hat. "How's your place?"

"Nothin' the good Lord won't help us mend. Stan and I were discussin' if you were ever comin' back home. Thought if that storm didn't keep ya away, at least the girl in Arizona had a hold on ya."

"Lizzy," he mumbled and scratched at his ever-growing unshaved beard. "What else has the good judge mentioned?"

Jeanna Ray waved her hand at him as though he were a horsefly. "Nothin' worth carryin' on about. You know, Stan and I've been married nearly forty-five years, and we know love when we see it. Or in this case, hear it."

"I'm not sure what you heard, but it must've been the wind." Gavin used his gloves to smack his palm. "If y'all need a hand with anythin', let me know. I best get back to cleanin' up."

"I know when I'm bein' shooed away." Jeanna Ray started to walk backward before spinning about like a teenager. When she got to the edge of the drive, she turned back around. "Shoot, I was supposed to invite ya for supper."

Gavin checked his cell phone. "Sounds good, six o'clock work?"

"Perfect."

And with that, Jeanna Ray was out of his line of sight, disappearing behind the upside-down minivan that belonged to the neighbor four houses over.

With Gavin's stomach full of charred hot dogs and mashed potatoes and gravy, he struggled to fall asleep. Jeanna Ray always managed to cook up something over her fire pit. He was in the opposite of a drowsy food coma. He was having food insomnia. All he could see when he shut his eyes was Aurora's beautiful face. The way the strands of hair blew across her cheek, causing her to constantly push them behind her ears, except when she had on her worn baseball hat that hid her golden-brown eyes. The urge to push the brim of the hat up so he could see them caused his hands to cramp, fighting off the memory.

He sat up in bed, the darkened house all around him. Not even the glow of a TV could be found. The power had been turned back on, but he had so much water damage he wasn't sure where to start, and using the power could be hazardous.

Gavin pulled on his boots and swiped his nearly dead cell phone off the nightstand.

The screen door squealed when he pushed it open and stepped out under the full moon's light. As he crossed his yard, he approached the back of his truck and lowered the tailgate. His back porch had been swept away, and there was no place to sit outside other than on the soggy grass.

Lying on his back in the truck bed, he gazed up at the white-as-flour moon, taking the time to notice the gray splotches and checked the time on his cell—11:20. That made it 9:20 in Arizona. Willa and Ava were probably just getting to bed, and Aurora would likely be doing dishes or relaxing with some wine. He pulled up her contact but didn't call. Instead, he exited out and went to the photo gallery. Since he'd returned, he found himself looking at the pictures at least twice a day.

A crunch of footsteps across the way caused him to sit up.

"Who's there?" he called out. "Make yourself known."

"Just me, Gavin," Jeanna Ray said, appearing in the moon's spotlight.

"Goodness, what are you doin' out?"

Jeanna Ray leaned against the truck's bed but didn't hop up.

"I think Stan put way too much paprika in those dogs, three antacids later, and I still feel like my chest is on fire." She crossed her arms. "The question is, what're you doin' up starin' at your phone?"

"How'd you see that far away to know what I'm doin'?" Gavin asked, leaning back and setting his phone on his knee.

"Doc sent me into Shreveport, and I had that laser surgery done on my peepers. Perfect vision." Jeanna Ray pressed her fingers together on her right hand like a chef about to kiss them after the perfect meal.

"Your vision can't see through my truck."

Jeanna Ray nodded her head. "I've lived enough of a life to know when a man is smitten. And when I came around your truck, I saw your phone in your hand. I can add two and two, young man." She waved her pointer finger at him.

He flipped his phone in his hand. "Can I ask you somethin'?"

"Shoot, kid."

He was sure he would regret this, but what the heck. "How did you know Stan was the one?" Gavin shook his head at the absurdity of such a question. For goodness' sake, he was a grown adult man, and here he was acting like a schoolboy with a crush.

A smile tweaked on Jeanna Ray's cheeks. "I couldn't stop thinkin' about him. I envisioned our future together every minute of the day. Thinkin' of what our life would be like and if he felt the same. What adventures we would have, how we could grow together, and support each other throughout life."

"And look at you two now." Gavin continued to rotate the phone in his hand.

"Now, yes, of course. I had no idea at the time if my dreams would come true. I could only hope that he would ask me to marry him and we'd live happily ever after. And my, did he drag his darn feet on that one. I think we carried on for over three years, which was a rather long time back then. My friends were datin' and gettin' engaged in a year."

"Was there anything that stood in your way?"

"I see what you're gettin' at, and no, we didn't have to deal with a distance of states between us. But Stan wasn't ready when I was ready, and that's why it took so long, in my opinion. Sometimes you have to let life run its own race, even if the rest of the runners have passed you by and the crowd has dispersed. All you can do is focus on the finish line."

"I guess I don't know what to do because I don't want to push her away. I don't think she's ready. I mean, I don't think she knows if she's ready. Either way, I'll wait. I'd wait for her to be ready."

"But you don't want to. Your heart is rushin' like you're about to have a heart attack if you don't get to be with her. And you're willin' to give up your life here?"

"Love is never as easy as cuttin' soft butter. I can't ask her to move, and I'm not sure I can bring myself to leave. But every time I think about her, everythin' here fades away." He rubbed his hand on his forehead—*even the nightmares of Mila and Jax*. "Yet, our roots are too deep to break them when push comes to shove."

"Love can be as cruel as a hurricane. You know it's headin' for ya, but you have no idea the damage it'll do until after the fact, and you can't prevent what it does to reshape your life."

Gavin tossed his head back, looking towards the moon. "So, what do you do?"

"Move west." Jeanna Ray snickered. "Just board up as best you can and pray it doesn't break your heart."

Gavin swung his legs back and forth over the tailgate, like a kid without a care in the world when in fact he had every care imaginable.

"But I'll give you some unsolicited advice and take it for what you want." She placed her hand on his knee. "We've been neighbors goin' on twenty-some years now, and I've never once seen you this wrapped up by a woman, even when that one with the Hollywood hair was over nearly every weekend. And I know you miss her and her little boy, but don't allow their ghosts to haunt you forever."

# Chapter 35

## Aurora

There was no way Aurora was going to fly out and see Gavin. Speaking with him face-to-face was not possible. At least that's what she reminded herself sixteen hours ago, just before she visited Elizabeth, got Gavin's address, and secured a ticket to Louisiana.

It was the first time she'd been away from her kids since Mike had passed, and the worry rested deep in her shoulders, pulling them down. But she didn't want to tell them why she was going away for two days, yet when Ava asked if she was going after Gavin like in the movies, the tears welled up in Aurora's eyes. She had no choice, then, to be honest. Aurora told Ava she was going to speak with Gavin about something important between adults. By the time she'd boarded the plane, Aurora had all but forgotten about the why and what. She could only think about how his arms felt around her and how comfortable she was with him. How much she needed him, needed to be near him. And these thoughts caused guilt to course through her veins for their future.

Allowing the rental car's GPS to guide her, she found herself on the road leading to Gavin's house, or by the looks of it, what might be left. The street was lined with leafless trees on both sides of the road. Many were ripped to shreds, their tops missing, split in half, or completely laid out. She couldn't wrap her mind around coming home to find *this*.

She hoped that surprising Gavin would be a welcomed occurrence; Aurora even packed a pair of work gloves to help him as much as he needed. There was nothing more fitting than to chat about the future while cleaning up the aftermath of the hurricane.

Yet, driving through the neighborhood it was nearly impossible to determine which house was which because the numbers were gone or hanging haphazardly, allowing nines to look like sixes.

But thankfully, she didn't need a house number to find Gavin's home. Aurora recognized his dirt-covered truck parked near the edge of a driveway ahead. As she slowed to turn off the road, she spotted a man on what was left of a home's roof.

She pulled the economy-sized rental car into the drive, parking next to his truck, and as she climbed from the vehicle, Gavin turned in her direction. His cowboy hat blocked her from seeing his eyes, but she didn't need to see them to remember how it felt when he looked at her.

"Howdy!" Aurora called up to him as she shut the car door.

"Aurora? Is that you?" Gavin reached the ladder and hurried down it.

He wiped his hands on the sides of his jeans as he stood in front of her. She smiled boldly and reached forward, hugging him. He smelled of lumber and soil. Aurora pulled away before she wanted to, yet she knew if she didn't step back that she might've stayed with her arms around Gavin for minutes.

"What the heck are you doin' here?" Gavin took his hat off, ran his hands through his hair, and then fidgeted with the brim, reminding her of Kevin Costner. "That came out wrong."

"No, sorry. I should've called or asked, or . . ." Aurora squeezed her hand around the keys. "I'm only here to find out if you came up with a nickname for me yet."

He chuckled and shook his head.

"Sorry, it was too forward of me to assume it could show up unannounced."

His hand reached out for her arm. "No, I'm surprised, is all. Is somethin' wrong?"

"Yes, very much so." Aurora swallowed the rock of a lump that'd formed in the back of her throat. There was really no good way to say what she needed to say or ask what she needed to ask.

He took her hand and led her to the back of his truck, lowering the tailgate. And because of her height, he lifted her onto it by holding her hips, and then joined her. Their knees touched, and it caused shivers to travel from Aurora's legs to her fingers. No matter how confused she was, she couldn't deny how being around Gavin made her feel alive.

He rubbed his hands back and forth on the top of his jeans as though he didn't know what else to do with them. Aurora set her hand over the top of his left hand and rested it there. Under his tough skin, she felt the firmness of the bones in Gavin's hands.

"I spent the entire flight trying to wrap my mind around what I was thinking—spending some proper alone time to process everything that happened over the last few weeks and also being a widow, dealing with the feelings that have engulfed me since he passed. With what I need and want. My heart has been doing so much flipping and flopping around that I'm pretty sure if I tripped on something, it'd throw it clear out my mouth."

196

Gavin turned his hand over, causing Aurora's palm to press against his. She could feel their heartbeats matching as they pulsed through the skin.

"I can't stop thinkin' about you," he breathed the words and turned to her.

Aurora focused on the view of destruction in front of them. She didn't even have to look at him to know that he was observing every little detail on her face. Aurora bit her lower lip, her cheeks flushing under the knowledge. She'd caught him staring many times during their adventures in Woolsey.

No matter how hard Aurora tried to force the words out, she didn't know the order they belonged in. Not knowing where to start, the tears fell faster than ever, and she leaned her head on Gavin's shoulder. She missed him more than she ever thought possible.

He slid his hand out from under hers and wrapped his muscular arm around her shoulder, pulling her closer to him. She wiped away her tears, but it didn't do any good, they continued to spill out. She knew what falling in love felt like. It was like the dance of a maple leaf drifting from the tree's safety to the ground below.

As though reading her mind, Gavin whispered, "I know you loved Mike. I know you miss him and don't know what to think right now. Any man you fall in love with—any good man—will respect what you and Mike had. Starting over, bein' in love again . . . for you, it must contain that mutual understandin.'"

She sat up, and his hand went back to rest on his knee. "It's unfair." Aurora closed her eyes. "What kind of man wants to be with someone that has to compete against the past?"

"I don't think you're lookin' at it from the right angle. It's not a competition. It's not about who you love more. Love is not a contest. We all love things differently." Gavin pointed past his disheveled home into the mess of trees in the backyard. "See way out there?"

"Not really. There are too many trees."

"Exactly. Just because I can't see beyond the trees doesn't mean I have a bad angle and can't love the view as much as my neighbor, Jeanna Ray, who can see over the tops of these trees because she has a two-story home. Our love for the view is different because our viewpoints are different, but one is not better than the other."

Aurora pondered this notion and took a deep breath, filling her nose with the scent of damped earth.

"How about we discuss this over some food? I'm hungry, and I have nothin' to offer you here." Without waiting for a response, Gavin hopped off the tailgate and held his hands out. Aurora grabbed them and used them to lower herself into the mud below.

She followed Gavin as he held tight to her hand around the truck to the passenger side.

He opened the door for her without a word, and she climbed in. By the time he got in on the driver's side, her seat belt was on.

"What are you in the mood for?" Gavin turned the key, and the engine vibrated alive.

"Whatever works best. I figured there wouldn't be many things open. I didn't even think about the impossibility of booking a hotel."

He glanced at the dashboard's clock. "Plenty of time before the sun sets on the day to worry about all that."

The truck eased out of the drive and onto the main road as the whisper of Alan Jackson came through the radio. The devastation of the hurricane hurt Aurora's heart as they passed by house after house. They were headed in a different direction than she'd come in on, and her eyes were drawn to what was left of a once (she could only assume) beautiful Jesser Parish.

Stoplights hung low and were out of order as cars waited for their turn, easing through the intersections. Some lights worked, and a few houses remained half-erect while others had big red Xs on the front of them. Roofs were missing or caved in by fallen trees. Stop signs were bent and twisted, and sides of houses were exposed.

"I can't imagine coming home to find my house like this." She pointed out the passenger window. "Would it be worse to come home to this or to stay and try to keep things safe? Prevent it, somehow?"

"Do you have a superpower I don't know about?"

She twisted her head in his direction. "What?"

"One that can stop the force of water?"

Aurora slumped forward and sighed a laugh. "I'm used to monsoons. I guess it's easier to prevent the damage from those. Park your car in a garage to prevent hail damage, don't drive in it." She bit her lower lip. "I should stop talking."

Gavin halted the truck at what remained of a four-way stop. "Never cease talkin'—at least to me. Now, I have a great spot in mind. My buddy runs the place, and they got off lucky without much damage. It might be the only restaurant close by that's up and runnin' like normal."

"Sounds perfect." Anything with Gavin sounded blissful. However, she wanted to discuss them, the kids, Arizona, dating, Louisiana, all things that were far from perfect. Her head spun with thoughts. In fact, it'd been spinning since day two of spending time with Gavin—how very *Sleepless in Seattle* long-distance romantically-tragic the whole thing appeared.

Aurora gazed out the window, losing track of time and thankfully thoughts, for at least a little bit. Louisiana was lush with greenery and flat as the eye could see. Obviously, they were heading further inland as the destruction of the hurricane lessened with each mile. White water towers marked small towns. Some held cell tower globes, notifying the name painted in green, black, or blue around it. A split-rail fence appeared to the right of the road, and they turned where a sign hung from a post read Bayou Winery.

The bare trees were still dense enough to block any view until they were nearly on top of a faded crimson barn east of a gravel parking lot.

"Is this okay?" Gavin pulled into an unmarked spot and shut off the truck.

"A winery is *always* okay." She climbed from the passenger seat and breathed deeply.

The air had a lovely floral fragrance, perhaps a mix of sweet water and honey. The path to the front door was lined with blossoming miniature bushes of flowers in creams and purples.

The barn had its doors opened, and the light from inside spilled onto her boots as they approached. Inside were wooden tables and mismatched chairs, and in the middle, a rectangle bar top displayed the wines. Thin barstools flanked around it, letting her know this was not only the restaurant but also the tasting area. A swinging door was off to the area's left, and the wooden walls showcased a history of artwork. Two sets of French doors were at the back end and opened to the vineyard beyond an expansive stone patio. A couple sat in the corner, unaware of them, while two women sat nearby, their purses slung over the back of the chairs and their lipstick leaving outlines on their wineglasses. They gave a smile and nod when they spotted her and Gavin.

A lady in a white button-down shirt popped her head up from behind the bar with a bottle of wine in each hand. "Gavin, how the heck are ya? Jim told me you'd be by once you were back in town." She set the bottles down and strolled over, giving Gavin a quick hug.

"Norma, I'm glad y'all are doin' well."

"And who's your pretty gal?"

Aurora smiled, feeling like she was a shy child receiving a compliment. "I'm Aurora." She eased her hand out.

Norma took it with both hands as she shook it. "Welcome. Y'all wanna sit inside or out? It's mighty good weather."

"I think we'll take a seat outside." Gavin stepped toward the French doors.

Norma swung around, swiped two menus off the counter, and used them to wave Aurora and Gavin to follow her.

They reached the patio to find a couple with a baby in a stroller off in the corner and picked a seat a few over. Gavin pulled out Aurora's chair, and Norma handed her a menu and then one to him as soon as he took his seat across from her.

"Can we start with my favorite?" Gavin asked, setting the menu down without looking at it.

"Absolutely. Aurora, would you also like a glass of our Bayou Blueberry? It's our best seller."

"Sure, that sounds delightful," Aurora announced, spotting the canopy of globe lights strung overhead.

"Menu's the same as always. I'll be back in a few." Norma took a step back and faced the other couple. "Everythin' alright over there?"

They nodded, and Norma was on her way back inside as Aurora looked over the menu.

"It's my favorite wine, maybe a little girly, don't tell anyone." Gavin folded his hands and set them on top of the menu.

"Your secret is safe," Aurora said as she inspected the menu. She'd had some cheese bunnies on the plane, but that had been it since she'd left Arizona.

"Would you like to share a charcuterie plate with me?" Gavin asked.

"Oh, that sounds perfect. I don't think I could decide between a pizza or a cheese plate." Aurora set the menu to the side of the table and looked onto the fields.

Unlike the wineries in Northern Arizona, where the vineyards were planted on short, steep, rocky hillsides—like an apartment with too many roommates—this winery's grapes were grown in flat rows one could mistake for the beginning of corn season in the outstretched fields. Behind the rows were trees of many different kinds; it looked like the land had received a sprinkling of seeds spread by an energetic toddler.

As she glanced to her right, another set of vineyard rows stretched up a hill surrounding a stately tree that would make one killer climb. Of course, just like Arizona, wineries during the fall meant dormant vines. But that didn't stop Aurora from picturing the beauty of what it might look like right at the peak of the picking season.

"It's beautiful here. And damp." She laughed and leaned back in her chair, crossing her arms. "You never notice how dry the desert is until you're sitting in the—"

"Bayou. Yep, it's swampy down here, but at least our skin is nice and moisturized. If the mosquitoes don't eat us alive."

"I'm surprised they don't have this patio screened in." Aurora glanced around as though maybe she'd missed something.

"That's what those are for." Gavin pointed to the edges of the area where large metal cylinders sat. "They catch most of the flying insects and allow for an unscreened view of the vineyard."

"Those actually work?"

"Either that or no one who comes here has yummy blood." Gavin adjusted his hat to block the sun from hitting his nose.

Aurora giggled and rubbed her hands together. Usually, she'd be smothering on lotion at least twice a day. And with that, she couldn't help but wonder for a second that maybe she could leave Woolsey and start her life over with the girls here. But as soon as the thought developed, it was wiped out by the legacy of her family's homestead.

Norma returned with two wineglasses filled halfway with deep red wine and set them directly in front of their silverware-wrapped napkins.

"We'll have the mixed meat platter with cheese." Gavin collected the menus and handed them to Norma.

"Comin' right up." She grabbed the menus and hurried off.

"Mixed meat platter *with cheese?*" Aurora leaned in and picked up her glass of wine.

"Sounds more macho to order it that way. Charcuterie sounds glamorous. To your first, and hopefully not last, trip to Louisiana." He held up his glass, and they clinked.

She put the glass to her lips and sipped the wine. It was a semi-dry merlot taste, and when she swallowed it, it left a sweet finish on the insides of her cheeks. "I don't want to be too forward, but I didn't fly all this way to ignore the reason I came."

Gavin set his glass down, and his vision fell to her lips and then back up to her eyes.

"I also don't want to be so bold as to assume that I'd be welcomed," she added.

"Then how about I go first?"

Aurora took a long sip of wine to help her through what was about to happen, good or bad.

# Chapter 36

## Gavin

He'd been practicing what to say since Aurora had unexpectedly shown up in his driveway. But going over every word and thought several times in a row, he now had no idea why it was so hard to say the words.

Their platter arrived, and his stomach nearly reached out of his body for a bite as Norma set two bread plates in front of them.

"Enjoy. You make a lovely couple. Gavin, I had no idea." She winked, and before he could correct her, not that he wanted to, Norma hurried off.

He was unaware of how hungry he'd become since his mind was focused on Aurora. Motioning for her to go first, he pushed his hands into his knees as though to keep from grabbing the food straight from the patter like a wild bear coming upon an open cooler.

Using the small three-pronged fork, she piled her plate with crackers, cubes of cheese, and some sliced prosciutto. Then she handed him the fork, and he stacked his small plate with more meat than cheese. Maybe if he kept his mouth continuously full of food, he could avoid putting what his heart was telling him out there.

"I can go first," Aurora started, wiping her fingers on her napkin.

"No." *Crap!* He gulped the wine. "I've not stopped thinkin' about you. I understand that if we were to be in a relationship, one of us would have to give up our life in the only home we've ever known. Now, I don't want to push you into anythin', even if we were neighbors, until you're ready. If you're ready. When you're ready." He wiped his palms on the top of his jeans and closed his eyes to keep his head from spinning any more than it was already. "Is it hot in here?"

"We're outside. It's in the sixties." Aurora tilted her head at him.

Gavin pinched his eyes closed. "Right. The humidity must be gettin' to me. I guess I got used to the desert."

"We got used to you being there. You're all the girls talk about and all I . . ." She wrapped her right hand around her wineglass but didn't pick it up. Then she slid her hand down the stem of the glass and brought it to her chest. "I might be confused about what to do next, with how I should feel. But one thing I do know is I'm falling . . . I'm . . ."

"I'm fallin' too." He reached his hand across the table, and she placed hers in his. "Is that why you come all this way?"

"I don't know how to be right, and I can't afford to be wrong. Because I don't know the answer, or at least the right answer." Her voice weakened with each word, and he hoped she didn't start crying. He hated when she cried because he couldn't fix what was wrong.

Gavin stood, picked up his chair, and moved it next to Aurora's. He took ahold of her hand and weaved it with his. "I can't ask you to leave Woolsey."

"And I would never ask you to leave your life here. I never thought I'd ever find anyone that made me feel the way you do. That made me realize I wasn't dead inside anymore.

205

You've helped me understand *I can* feel again. I only wish I knew what to do."

Though holding her hand, he felt her shiver. As he pulled her close, she gazed up and him, and he couldn't help himself. He couldn't stop himself as he lowered his lips to hers and kissed her.

When they parted, they said nothing. But Gavin reached for his wine, and he stayed sitting next to Aurora as they ate in silence, looking out at the view. What worried him most of all was not knowing what they should do now. Yet again, he didn't have an answer.

Other than George Strait's vocals, they'd remained silent the entire drive back.

"Are there any jobs available in Woolsey?" Gavin pulled into his driveway, shut off the truck, but the keys remained in the ignition.

"Little things here and there pop up, but most only last a day or two, nothing long term in town for construction. Jobs would be available in Cactus City, and that would mean a commute."

It was a reminder he already knew the answer to. And her nonprofit company wouldn't need him enough to allow for yearly income. He could commute. Yet, it came down to if he could leave all he knew, all he had. Was she someone worth leaving everything behind for? Was she the one?

"Do you want to give us a try?" Aurora's delicate voice broke through his thoughts.

"I can't ask you to do that."

"I'm not asking you what you want me to do; I'm asking if you want to see where we go, together." She turned to him, tears streaming down her cheeks, and he took his thumb and wiped them away. And as he did, she closed her eyes and kissed the palm of his hand.

Gavin eased his eyes closed as her lips met the skin of his hand. It was most definitely hot, but it wasn't the weather.

Aurora squeezed his hand with hers. "I'm falling in love with you. I don't know if it's too soon. I don't know if it makes me a bad person. I don't know if it's okay for my girls. But Gavin, I can't control it or how quickly it happened. And it makes me feel so confused and excited at the same time. I want us to be together. I need us to be together. And that's why I'm giving up everything I have in Arizona."

"Wait." He pulled back, and her hand dropped his hand. "No, you can't do that. I won't let you."

"I can't let you give up your life to come all the way out to some small town with no employment prospects."

"And I can't let you move your girls away from everythin' they know, let alone your family home."

"But I'm willing to do it for you, for us. I've heard you talk about the community here, and you might have a house in need of repairs, but your house is really all of Jesser Parish."

"I don't want you to give up everythin' you have in Woolsey."

"What do you want then?" Aurora's eyes scrunched, and a crease between her brows wrinkled.

Gavin rested both hands on the top of the steering wheel, his thumbs tapping the air around it. When he breathed deeply through his nose, Gavin realized his truck now smelled of Aurora. If they didn't work out, he'd have to sell it because he wouldn't be able to get her or the perfect apple and honey scent out of it or his mind. "I want you enough to give it all up."

"I'm not letting you give up your life for us. I won't be that woman." Aurora popped open the door and fumbled her keys from her purse.

He climbed from the truck and hurried around, but she was already at her rental car. "I want you."

"Not that way." She kept shaking her head, facing the driver's side. Gavin reached out and pressed his hands onto the frame of the side window, on either side of Aurora.

She spun around and was met with his close proximity, but he didn't move his hands to her shoulders. Instead, he allowed the air between them to stir with tension, which only caused Gavin's heart to race faster.

"Are you listenin'? I want to be with you." He pressed his palms harder into the frame. "I want to give it all up for you." Gavin reached one of his arms out towards his home, his land, and his history but quickly put them back on the car.

Aurora looked around. "I can't ask you to do that."

"You're not askin' me. I'm doin' it." Gavin moved his hands to her shoulders, pressing gently.

She shook her head. "This was a bad idea, all of it. I can't do this. I'm sorry."

Aurora spun around as his hands fell from her shoulders. He stumbled backward, shaken by her response. She flung open the car door, and before he could blink, the rental car was in reverse and backing out of his driveway.

His mind raced as he made fists. Should he go after her? Gavin had never been in love like this. His heart thumped in his chest. "I'm in love."

"You better go after her!" Jeanna Ray hollered across the way.

"Dang it." He had no choice but to chase after her.

He jumped in his truck, and fumbled with the keys, dropping them on the floorboard below. It was getting dark outside, and the inside of the cab was not light enough to see. His hands felt around frantically until they located a pointy end and snatched them up. With his fingers trembling, he went to shove the key in, turning it so hard that he felt it bend, nearly breaking it off.

Gavin threw the truck into reverse and revved out of the driveway. He spotted Jeanna Ray standing on her front porch, pointing in the direction Aurora went.

"I love her!" he yelled out the rolled-down window.

"Don't tell me that. Tell her!" Jeanna Ray hollered.

"Where is she goin'?" he asked himself as he sped down the road, trying to catch up to her. "Where is she?"

Aurora hadn't been too far in front of him, so why had he not seen her yet? There were still stacks of debris littering the side of the road that even familiar places looked new to him. Nightfall darkened the sky quickly. He had to find her. He had to make it all right.

# Chapter 37

## Aurora

Aurora had zero idea where she was headed, but she was speeding. She had the pedal down far enough that if she hit a ramp, she'd be able to do the same jump as the General Lee in *Duke's of Hazard*.

She took a turn off the road to what she thought was towards the interstate, but it was clearly not as the pavement turned to gravel. Aurora tried to spot a water tower to give her some sort of direction, but she had no idea what she was looking for to begin with. She hadn't booked a hotel, and while she could use the GPS, she didn't have a clue as to where she wanted to go, only that she wanted to run away.

The sun had dipped behind the bank of bare trees a while ago, causing the sky to fade into black. As she became lost in thought, Aurora drove by a sign that might have helped her gain some direction had she not caught the blurry end of it.

The road grew narrower, and the gravel turned to mud as the telephone poles all leaned at an angle over the street. Trees became denser with each mile as the street felt like it was soaking into the rubber grooves of her tires. Aurora didn't see a house or another street sign as she continued on. She'd been turned around before, but never like this.

Deciding the best thing to do was circle back, Aurora gauged she had enough room and slowed down to start her 180-degree turn. But with the only light being her headlights, Aurora misjudged where the mud road and muddy swamp joined.

Turning the wheel, she directed the car to the left, causing the vehicle's front to lean a bit forward. Keeping the wheel taut beneath her grip didn't prove to matter because even with the steering wheel turned to the left, the car kept going straight.

Shutting off the radio and rolling down the window, Aurora noticed her front driver's side wheel was stuck in the mud. And this meant the passenger side's front wheel must also be stuck. With each punch of the gas pedal, the wheels spun, pushing the front of the vehicle deeper into the swamp that had become the side of the road.

"Crap-o-crap!" Aurora hit the steering wheel and pressed her head back into the headrest.

She picked up her cell phone to call for a rescue, but she had no idea where she even was to direct someone to her, let alone who to call.

"The internet, duh." But when she went to open the app, her phone flashed an empty battery sign before going completely dark.

Tossing the phone on the passenger seat, she got out of the car. The dip the vehicle was in ran the entire length of the road, and the swampy water was up to the wheelbase. There was no way she'd be driving out of there unless the car was towed.

Aurora glanced up and down the road in both directions. Some pine trees flanked both sides just past the ditch and stretched beyond the view. Then, feeling herself lowering, she looked down to see her boots had sunk into the mud too.

"Ugh!" She yelled and turned her head up to the sky.

Shifting her feet in her boots, she stiffened her foot, lifting it to step ahead, but the boots remained stuck as she jerked forward, crashing to the earth below. Mud-covered her knees, socks, and hands. Aurora closed her eyes and pressed her lips together. Not only was she lost, but now she was covered in wet, stinky mud, and without the sun, it had grown cold.

"Snakes, there must be snakes out here." She smacked the back of her leg as though she could already feel them slithering upon her.

While remaining on her knees, she reached for the car's door handle to hang onto something to get herself upright. She leaned forward more and gripped the side mirror for leverage. Then, pushing her lower body up and pulling with her upper body, she put all her weight on the mirror, and when she was just about upright, the mirror snapped off. Aurora stumbled backward toward the ditch, plopping down unceremoniously with the casing in her hand.

"This is the worst."

She had no strength to even bother getting up. With the mirror in her hand, she held it up, barely able to see in the darkness, but she knew what was there—swollen eyes from crying and splashes of mud across her cheeks and in her hair.

Light from a vehicle, higher up, possibly a truck, headed her way. She dropped the mirror and scrambled forward. She needed to flag it down. On all fours, she pushed her bottom up in the air like a poorly planned downward dog yoga pose.

Just as she stood upright, the lights were feet away and slowed to a stop. Aurora gave a wave and hoped whoever it was had good intentions.

Going from blinding lights to pitch black caused blue rings in her vision, and she squinted as someone climbed out.

"Coyote, you're the last person I expected to rescue in Louisiana," a familiar man's voice echoed in the cold air.

"Gavin?" she asked as the figure stepped forward, and her eyes had finally adjusted, allowing her to be able to see him. "Who's *Coyote*?"

As though noticing the muddy mess she was in, he hurried to her and clutched her elbows firmly. "You are, it's your nickname."

"Why?"

"Because you're adventuresome, bold, and persistent. Plus, you saved one's life."

She smiled, grabbing onto his arms in return. "Oh, be careful. I'm covered," she warned. "I'm so sorry for running."

Apparently, he didn't care about getting dirty as he brushed the mud off her cheek with the back of his fingers. Before she could say a word about the entire matter, his lips were on hers as their mud-covered arms wrapped around each other. She moved her arms to his neck, pulling herself closer to him. Gavin's lips were warm on hers, and her heart raced, pressing against his firm chest.

When he pulled away, he said, "I don't want you givin' up your life. I want to be with you. I'll find a way to make it work in Woolsey. If you're willin' to give us a try."

"I told you, can't let you do that." She pressed her forehead against his chest and then looked up at him.

He smacked the back of his neck. "The mosquitoes are bad out here. Let's talk about this once we get out of the sucklin' blood bath."

He guided Aurora to the passenger side of his truck and once she was inside, Gavin wasted no time jumping in and slamming his door.

She had no idea how gross she looked, covered in mud and smelling of moldy earth. "If we don't work, I'll never forgive myself for causing you to give up everything for me."

"Way to put the shrimp before the grits."

She scrunched her face up, confused. "I've never had a grit."

"We'll have to fix that real quick." He smirked. "Aurora, I . . . I . . ." He dragged his hand around the back of his neck.

"I love you, Gavin." The words nearly shook from her lips, but they were true. They were the most honest she'd been with her feelings in a long time.

He reached out his right hand, slid it behind her upper back, and pulled her toward him again, kissing her lips until she couldn't catch a breath. Then, withdrawing just enough, he rested his forehead on hers. "I love you, too, Aurora. You're not the only one who didn't think they could ever fall in love again after a loss."

"Loss?" Aurora's heart went from joyful to sullen in half a second.

She observed Gavin's eyes as they lowered, glanced out the driver's window, and back at her.

"I'd like to share with you my loss." He cleared his throat. "That is, how I lost Mila and Jax."

Aurora took her hand and placed it on the side of Gavin's face and gave him a sorrowful smile. "Thank you for trusting me."

"For trustin' us."

# Epilogue

## Thanksgiving

Delightful chatter buzzed in Aurora's hanger. Lillian, the main chef of the Thanksgiving meal, held the spot at the head of the table. Camden, Trinity, and Jolie were to her right. Then R. J. and Elizabeth followed in the chairs to the left, along with Aurora, Ava, and Willa.

"This is going to be scrumptious!" Ava called out, standing on her knees on her chair.

"She's on S words in school this week." Aurora motioned for Ava to sit on her bottom.

The afternoon sun provided a warm glow over the plastic tables and residents eager to eat, as Aurora stood so she could see over the top of the heads.

"So, are we ready?" Lillian asked, holding the knife above the golden turkey. "Wait, where's Gavin and Charlie?"

"He's getting the mac and cheese cups from the oven," Aurora announced as Gavin appeared at the opening of the hangar.

"Sorry, y'all." Gavin set the platter of steaming cheesy noodles near the green bean casserole and took a seat nearest Willa.

Aurora beamed a smile in his direction, and he gave her a wink, scooting in his chair. She was not only glad he could be here for Thanksgiving but also that he'd be living in Woolsey full time come the new year.

A rumble of a worn 1982 Dodge Ram D-Series filtered into the hangar. After the slam of a solid frame door, Charlie entered, clutching a paper bag in each hand.

"Happy Thanksgiving!" Charlie lifted both bags equally up to midline.

"Happy Thanksgiving!" Everyone cheered.

Charlie set the bags near the buffet table. "Terribly sorry to be holding the supper up. I had to give Alexander a hand over at the library."

"The library is closed." Lillian remained standing, her eyes puzzled.

Charlie removed several wrapped items dressed in leaves and brown bows. Then he spun around, silence in the air, along with the scent of turkey, gravy, and warm bread.

"Yes, it's closed. I owed him . . . a favor." He held up one of the presents. "Just a little something for the kids after we eat."

"Thank you, Charlie," Trinity stated from her chair. "You didn't have to do that."

Charlie approached the table. "It's my pleasure. Shall I sit here?"

He was standing behind the empty chair that was nearest to Lillian. Aurora had specifically set the table to allow Lillian and Charlie to sit together. She couldn't shake the feeling that Desert Guy was Charlie for some reason.

"Yes, please." Lillian smiled coyly. "That was thoughtful of you to bring something for the kids."

Aurora watched as Lillian and Charlie kept their eyes glued to each other, and she noticed that every other resident, minus the children, noticed precisely the same thing.

After everyone stacked their plates with food, filling them to the edges, the chatter started about their upcoming Christmas plans and the mouthwatering food.

"How's your house coming along?" Camden directed his question toward Gavin.

Gavin rested his fork on the side of his plate. "A lot slower than I'd like. But I think everything should be set by Christmas time."

"And then you'll put it up for sale?" Camden paused, his butter knife gilding over his roll.

Gavin glanced over at Aurora as she brought a bite of sweet potato to her lips. "Actually, I'm keeping the house as our vacation home. We plan on having many trips out there."

"What a great idea," Trinity chimed. "We can watch the girls when you're gone."

"That won't be necessary. They'll be family vacations." Gavin's face beamed with joy.

Aurora couldn't wait for their first trip together, even if they weren't engaged and not an official family by standard terms. She was in a place in life where she could welcome each day as it came with the sun. There were no expectations of how their life would go together, only that they would put each other first and allow love to guide their path.

As they continued to enjoy their Thanksgiving meal, a hummingbird fluttered inside. Aurora spotted it and watched it fly near her and the girls, pausing in the air. It appeared to be looking at them and then toward Gavin. The hummingbird did a little dip lower and then higher before buzzing back out of the hangar.

"That was odd," Gavin said, holding a chunk of cranberry bread in his hand.

Aurora closed her eyes for a second and smiled knowing it wasn't odd at all.

# The End

I hope you enjoyed your time in Woolsey. I'd be super-duper appreciative if you would spare a minute and let me know if you loved the story, or not via a review.

THE FINAL BOOK IN THE HEARTS OF WOOLSEY SERIES

**This year's library Christmas celebration will be one for the books.**

A Desert Rivalry

# Acknowledgments

Thank you to Linda Martin, Durene Adams, Piepie Baltz, Sandy Herzog, Sherri Bailey, Joyce Stewart, Starla DeKruyf, Annette G. Anders, Lissa Ruck, Patty Bulick, Betty Mitchell, Sandy Ebbinga, and Lisa Small. Y'all are always so excited to read my latest novel and I love you for it!

A big hug to my *Happy PAWS Readers* ~ Sam Alvarez, Robin Batterson, Rachel Blackburn, Carol Harris, JoAnna McGarvie, JoDena Pysher, Elaine Sapp, Carrie Thompson, Lisa Wetzel.

Thank you to my editor Krista Dapkey for your amazing editing skills.

I KNOWWWWW I'm forgetting people, so please, if you don't see your name, just write it in. Take a pen and add it, I've left you space. If it's an ebook, screenshot it and add it in photo editor.

I'd like to thank _____, who I forgot to mention because Ransom needed another round of fetch, and then he needed a treat, and so by the time I got back to my computer I'd forgotten.

# About the Author

Savannah Hendricks (born in California, raised in Washington, and resides in Arizona) is a full-time social worker and fills as much of her weekends as possible with writing. She loves all things dog-related and has a passion for red wine. Savannah enjoys gardening, baking, and creating yummy recipes. You'll often find her hollering at the TV during restoration shows when they paint over red bricks.

If you'd love a digital personalized autograph or bookplate, you can request one by visiting: savannahhendricks.com
Please discover more about Savannah by interacting with her on:

Instagram: savannahhendricks_author
Facebook: AuthorSavannahHendricks

# Also By Savannah

## SAVANNAH HENDRICKS

*Where Does "I Love You" Go?*
*The Needle-less Christmas Tree & Other Tree Tales*
*Winston Versus the Snow* (Multi-Award-Winning)
*Nonnie and I* (Available in English, Spanish & Bilingual)